As if he had been reading her thoughts, Lord Ballington said, "There are many people of our acquaintance who believe that sexual fantasies should remain in the imagination, that to live them is dangerous. I am not of their breed and neither are you, darling. Indulge, I say. Indulge and enjoy. The harm is in repression."

She laughed softly, throatily, promise, as always, suggested by the sound. "You have a certain *persuasive* way with words."

*Frannie, Lady Ballington, is about to begin a year-long odyssey into sex and sensuality. In both the New and the Old World, her wildest carnal desires will be indulged, for she is young, beautiful and rich. Nothing is impossible . . .*

G000146736

# FRANNIE:

## Lady Ballington – her memoirs

## Anon

Futura

A Futura Book

ISBN 0 7088 3760 3

Reproduced, printed and bound in Great Britain by
Hazell Watson & Viney Limited
Member of BPCC plc
Aylesbury Bucks

Futura Publications
A Division of
Macdonald & Co (Publishers) Ltd
Greater London House
Hampstead Road
London NW1 7QX

A member of Maxwell Pergamon Publishing Corporation plc

For Jamie Todesco,
with a slightly crooked smile

'Commit
The oldest sins the newest kind of way.'
  – *Henry IV Part Two*, William Shakespeare.

'There is no such thing as an immoral book.
Books are well written, or badly written.'
                                        – Oscar Wilde.

# 1
# In My Beautiful Balloon

To any sexually average female the vibrations
communicating from Heathrow Airport tarmac
through rubber tyres, into the exquisitely honed body
of a Lear jet and, finally, via Lady Ballington's specially
designed, cashmere upholstered seat to her superbly
rounded, silk and satin-clad haunches, would have
represented nothing more than the stirrings of a
powerful mechanical beast gathering momentum
enough to lift itself into the heavens.

But for Frannie, Lady Ballington, the tremors of her
aircraft spoke to her, as exterior stimuli so often did,
directly through her crotch; during those final, crucial
seconds when the jet approached its lift-off speed its
projection of controlled, masculine power implied an
over-riding emotion to her: a sexual one. The Lear jet
was a sleek, tightly muscled male and her ladyship
fantasized lifting her skirt, opening her legs, and
having it fuck her. Take-off was the point of relief, for
the plane at least, the heavy vibrations at once replaced
by subtle, barely noticeable ones. Rested now in
comparatively effortless flight, the machine had had its
orgasm, but Frannie, damp between her legs, her
white, fleshy inner thighs rubbing together with
diminishing vigour, had not quite made it.

Frannie Jones Ballington (the 'Jones' was a relic from
a somewhat humbler life, which she could not bring
herself to drop upon marrying the middle-aged,

7

flamboyant Lord Ballington three days after her seventeenth birthday) was starting on the first leg of what was planned to be a long and especially adventurous holiday, the almost countless Ballington millions guaranteeing that she need spare no expense, however eccentric her whims. Nestling amongst her luggage was a large, oblong handbag which doubled as a video camera, its lens unobtrusive among half a dozen other glass discs which served as decoration. It was the most sophisticated, miniaturised infra-red camera available and was equipped with an ultra-sensitive sound recording system capable of picking up whisperings between sheets and reproducing them with a fidelity keen enough for a cinema screen.

'To us, and the last eight perfectly splendid years.' Immaculate in a burgundy smoking jacket set off by a floppy velvet bow which on most men of his age would have appeared pretentious but which on him managed to convey an air of old world gallantry, Lord Ballington raised his Waterford crystal glass and sipped appreciatively at the contents – a Chateauneuf du Pape, a wine as well matured and graceful as himself. His young wife's eyes danced greenly and amused at him through the flames of the two, six-pronged, silver candelabra which spaced the table into three exactly equal parts, and cast shadows on a banquet spread solely for the two of them.

Frannie's tongue traced a delicate line around her eminently kissable, softly erotic lips, adding a temporary gloss to the pale pink lipstick. She responded to the toast with a little, crooked, suggestive smile, resting her elbow on the table and tipping the base of her glass in his direction, but saying nothing.

Lord Ballington toyed thoughtfully with his grouse flown especially down from Scotland that morning; the delicate flesh fell cleanly away from the bone.

Before sampling the bird he remarked, 'You know, darling, I was rather apprehensive at first, for quite a long while after the wedding.'

'*Were* you? You never let it show.' Frannie's voice was just enough on the husky side to be unobtrusively sexy, the sort of voice which turns a man on over the telephone.

'No. It was a natural worry of course. You seventeen, me forty-three.'

'And now you're fifty-one. What of it?' She tried a morsel of grouse. 'Delicious!'

'Me at fifty-one, you mean?'

She gave him a serious look, shaking her head so that her long, full blonde hair bounced across bare, shapely shoulders. 'That too. You're still the most attractive man I know.'

Pleased, he smiled boyishly. In the candlelight Victor Ballington appeared far younger than he was, unusual in a man with half a lifetime's studied self-indulgence behind him. Studying him in the candlelight, Frannie was reminded of the dashing Clark Gable, just as she had been the first time they had met quite by accident sharing a taxi on a filthy London evening. He said, 'You've given me a big slice of your youth.'

'And you've given me *life*. Good God, Victor, I don't give a hoot for age. I stopped groping around with kids just after my sixteenth birthday. If you remember, my steady date before you wasn't much younger than you were then. Thirty-eight.'

Victor Ballington smiled again. 'Remember? I can hardly forget! That damned stuntman character. The one who taught you sexual tricks I couldn't believe in a girl of your age.' He chuckled. 'When you stopped seeing him he threatened me with all sorts of excruciating ways of dying.'

'And then you bought him off. So easy. The man had

no balls after all, despite his sexual prowess.' Frannie drained her glass and instantly a liveried butler who had been hovering in the shadows materialised to top it up. She raised it. 'I propose another toast. To sex. To sexual freedom, and to all our future adventures together.'

'I'll drink to that, but with an additional clause.' He paused. 'To our future adventures – together *and* apart.'

'*Apart*, darling? But we've never had sex with other people without us *both* joining in.' But she seemed only mildly surprised, and not at all shocked.

'No, we haven't. But don't you think it's about time we did? Broaden our horizons, wouldn't you say?'

Once again Frannie wetted her lips. Her soft green eyes narrowed. 'Do you really think it would be *wise*?'

'I'll tell you *exactly* what I think. We are two highly sexual beings, you and I. Much more so than the average person. You're virtually insatiable, and the same goes for me – which continues to surprise me as I grow older. I swear, every year I get hornier. So, given the fact that we seem to be made for each other in every way outside of sex too, that we are superbly compatible, I think our mutual bonds are too strong for any extra-marital sexual activity to break them.'

'Carry on. Convince me.'

He washed down a mouthful of grouse with wine. 'I believe that – to put it in the vernacular – screwing around a bit could bring us even closer together – in the telling.'

'Mmm.' Apprehensive at the prospect, Frannie nevertheless found that the consideration of it aroused her. She had had plenty of fantasies of being in wild sexual situations without her husband present, even whilst indulging in wild sexual situations *with* him there. The reality suggested possibilities as unlimited as her sexual drive.

As if he had been reading her thoughts, Lord Ballington said, 'There are many people of our acquaintance who believe that sexual fantasies should remain in the imagination, that to live them is dangerous. I am not of their breed and neither are you, darling. Indulge, I say. Indulge and enjoy. The harm is in repression.'

She laughed softly, throatily, promise, as always, suggested by the sound. 'You have a certain *persuasive* way with words.'

'Then you agree with me. Excellent!' He clapped his fine-boned, perfectly manicured hands together and the butler reappeared. 'Another bottle, I think, Charles. We must celebrate more than our wedding anniversary. As you have, no doubt, overheard.'

The butler bowed briefly and faded away, his pale, drawn features inscrutable.

'You think all of our fantasies should be lived? Each and every one?' There was the hint of delicious anticipation in Frannie's voice.

'Where's the harm? Let the body live what the mind invents. Remember last year's anniversary party? You'd been whispering in my ear for weeks before, during our most intimate moments, that you were pretending there were two blacks in bed with us.'

'And you went ahead and hired two black studs for that night. God, did the three of you …' She shivered at the memory and cupped her full breasts together with both hands as her thoughts sent a delicious tremor down her spine.

Charles, the butler, arriving with a freshly opened bottle while she was still in that attitude, kept all expression from his face as he topped up their glasses.

'Her Ladyship is remembering the two black gentlemen who joined our table last anniversary, Charles. Pretty obvious she had a *most* enjoyable night, wouldn't you agree?'

11

Aware of what was required of him, Charles glanced briefly at Frannie whose head was tilted slightly back, her eyes closed, her hands still on her breasts. 'Apparently, sir,' he remarked dutifully, before fading once again into the shadows.

'So, Frannie, you see that *indulging* that fantasy, which for many would prove to be, to say the least, an immense cultural shock, for us provided a superbly enjoyable night of sex, and exquisite memories. I reiterate – where's the harm?'

'Where indeed?' Frannie whispered, opening her eyes and giving her breasts an apparently reluctant final squeeze. 'I say, do you *have* to turn me on like this, bang in the middle of dinner?'

'It's not difficult. You are possessed, my darling, of the classic dirty mind.'

She ignored that. '*And* in front of Charles.'

'It's hardly the first time you've been turned on in front of the butler. Another fantasy – it adds to your enjoyment knowing he's listening. In any case, he hears and sees far more than you imagine.'

She pushed her plate away and Charles appeared again. 'I'm suddenly not hungry.' She watched the man pick up the plate and added, 'Not for food.'

'Well, at least have the pudding, Fran. A special banana flambé with a most respectably aged Napoleon brandy. After that –' he paused, eyeing her suggestively – 'After that you must satisfy that other appetite which has substituted for your hunger – in any way you think fit.'

During the dessert he sprang his big surprise, telling her quite off-handedly, as if he were discussing no more than a day trip in the country, of his extraordinary plans for this year's anniversary present, numbing her with the enormity of them.

She was to take an extended holiday without him. His private jet and an unlimited expense account were

12

to be at her disposal for the following three months. She was to travel wherever in the world she desired, but with one constant objective: sex. Sex at every opportunity and in as many combinations as possible. She would be provided with the most expensive sound and vision recording equipment available and wherever and whenever possible she would record the things which happened to her for their mutual enjoyment upon her return to the ancestral home at Stratton Castle. He, meanwhile, intended to go slumming, visiting the sleazier parts of British cities in search of adventure of his own. Lord Ballington had left no detail unplanned, not even a medical one; the risk of contracting a sexually transmitted disease during the course of such activities would be high. He had consulted with a Harley Street specialist on those matters and they were to be immunised, provided with as much protection as modern medical science was able to give.

He left Frannie breathless. Already quite heady from the wine, she nevertheless polished off two glasses of brandy after a second course of banana flambé.

He remarked at her silence. 'You haven't said very much.'

'Merely stunned. Well, look. You've been planning it for a while, it's your surprise. You're used to the idea by now. For me itsh –' she slurred the word, her first sign of having drunk a little too much. 'It's quite something to absorb just like that Victor. If you see what I mean.'

'Quite. But you'll soon get used to it.' He finished his own brandy, waving Charles away as he reached for the bottle. 'There's one thing I forgot to tell you. Important little detail. Besides, naturally, your personal maid, you'll be taking a security man with you. Well, a bodyguard really. One of the best. There's always the possibility of your needing to be extracted from a tricky situation. Gregory will always be close by, at the other end of a beeper, bleeper, whatever the damned things are called.'

'Gregory?'

He grinned. 'Unconvincing name for a bodyguard, I agree. But he's the works. Ex-SAS sergeant. I'll be having my back watched, too. His name fits the job. It's Bert.'

'You don't say?' She traced an invisible line on the tablecloth. 'Er, when is all this supposed to begin?'

'Couple of days. Give you a chance to pack, et cetera.'

'And where's the first stop?' She was speaking quietly, deliberately, trying not to let the alcohol interfere with her words, whilst a delicious feeling of excitement and anticipation of the sexual unknown spread warmth throughout her body and heat between her legs.

'That's up to you. Wherever you feel most comfortable. Somewhere you know quite well, at first, I should think. Paris maybe, the Côte d'Azure, Marbella, New York, Rome.'

'And how do I get into these adventures?'

'Don't even think about it. Make yourself available darling. They'll get into you.'

'You can say that again,' She whispered, *very* suggestively.

'Into you. Into your knickers and into you.' Lord Ballington, a tightness in his throat, a hardening at his groin, rose now and walked slowly down the length of the table towards his gorgeous wife. His eyes never leaving hers, he said quietly, 'You may go now, Charles. Thank you very much.'

He was standing above her, facing her, gazing down into deep, creamy cleavage, breasts straining at vermillion silk, reaching his aesthetic hands into the bosom of the dress, unfolding it, exposing pink, erect nipples, toying with them. 'How do you want me?'

'I'm coming already.' She reached for his zipper. 'I want to suck you. I want to suck your prick. Suck you right off. Cock in my mouth. *Cum* in my mouth.'

The zipper slowly, slowly sliding down. Fumbling with the top button. Insistent, searching hands; behind him, sliding into the waistband, under his pants, squeezing his buttocks, the ball of her finger tracing the cleft, momentarily pressing into his anus, then hands pulling his trousers and pants together half way down his thighs.

'Give me your cum.' Her voice at her deepest, trailing off into one of her fantasies. 'I'm going to swallow the cum from your big, fat, *black* balls.'

He was used to this particular fantasy; he had introduced her to it. His cock throbbing, fully exposed, standing, massive, the balls heavy underneath it. She rolls it against her cheek with one hand, carresses his balls with the other. Then she takes his cock deeply into her warm, wet mouth, sucking hungrily at it, making him groan as his buttocks tighten and his knees sag. It won't last long, he's fired himself right up with his story of delights to come. She doesn't *want* it to last long, she's ready to cum herself and, as she feels the familiar tension in him which preceeds those final, ecstatic moments of explosion, an incredible wave of orgasm begins to take hold of her body, her mind. He supresses a shout as his balls begin to empty, gritting his teeth, a strangled, animal sound coming from him as his sperm spurts and spurts and spurts into her delightful, willing mouth and she is swallowing it and the act of swallowing it accompanies and extends her own, totally self-consuming, orgasm.

His cock in her mouth a long time after, softening as they live the aftermath of sexual explosion. Finally she releases it with a sigh of replete satisfaction, licking the drips which continue to ooze from its head before he sinks to his knees and buries his face in her gown, at her crotch.

At the slightly ajar door to the banquet room, Charles, the butler, who does indeed, as Lord Ballington had earlier remarked, see more than Frannie imagines, his erect cock poking through red velvet trousers, his face as expressionless as ever, but the eyes closing as he silently spills his copious seed over a seventeenth-century Persian rug.

The plane nosed its way upwards, banking into the gloom of the several thousand feet cloud cover which so frequently lies like a carpet of doom over the English countryside. Unbuckling her safety belt, the sexual stimulation caused by take-off fading into a damp memory, Frannie lit a cigarette. To smoke was a rare event with her; she was trying to assuage the slight nervousness which was due to more than the normal squirm of apprehension she felt when airborne. First stop, New York, she had decided, once the idea of a journey into sexual adventure had finally taken a hold of her. New York, bustling, busy city of cities where free, abandoned sex was taken totally in its stride, a world of live sex shows, erotic films and luxurious clubs for determined swingers, a world which she had never failed to enjoy, the pace good and fast, stirring her into a keen sense of wakefulness, of being, after the relaxed contrast of life at Stratton Castle.

But without Victor? – She knew many of the places to go where she would meet the right crowd – greedy, restless people constantly on the look-out for new bodies to couple with, new minds to get into – but the apprehension she was feeling was of treading that road alone; she had not explored *any* sexual avenue without her husband in eight years, despite being the willing and eager partner in some pretty kinky activities.

Through the window, no comfort. A thick, murky

grey of impenetrable depth, almost scary. Water droplets, a life of their own, hovering and jerking across the glass.

Behind her, the massive Gregory, puffing on a freshly lit cheroot and leafing through a girlie magazine. Gregory with his protectionist box of tricks and his nimble, determined mind. If necessary the square-chinned, square-shouldered, square-brained Gregory could turn himself into a coldly efficient fighting machine; if necessary Gregory would kill.

And the bodyguard's instructions were precisely that. If things ever even began to appear dangerous for Lady Ballington on this trip he was to kill first and ask questions later. Or, rather, forget the questions and get her and him the hell out of there. Of course, such a situation was unlikely to arise. But it just might.

Gregory was prohibited from approaching her ladyship sexually. He could look but he was not allowed to touch, the relationship *must* remain at a purely professional level; there in lay her safety. These instructions were perfectly well understood by Frannie, who, being Frannie, whilst able to resist sexual temptation if she really had to, could nevertheless not help speculating on the size of this bear of a man's organ.

Across the aisle from Gregory was Matilda, Frannie's personal maid. Thirty-four year old Matilda of the bi-focal glasses and the prematurely greying hair in the severe bun and the shapeless pin-striped two-piece who, when she stripped off her clothes, untied her hair, removed her glasses and applied some make-up was transformed into the plump, lascivious object of sex who had often been used unashamedly by Frannie and Victor. Matilda who, more scared of flying than most, dreading the prospect of flying halfway around the world in the following three months, sat with her hands clasped tightly together, clenched between

17

tensed knees, her bespectacled eyes darting occasional nervous, furtive little glances across the aisle at Gregory's magazine.

Suddenly, unexpectedly, blindingly – England had not experienced the phenomenon in more than a month – sunlight. The elegant aircraft broke through the cloud layer and slid into the sparkling air above it, the cloud magically transformed from filthy, ominous, suffocating stuff to a snowy-white cotton carpet which stretched beneath them in every direction as far as the eye could see.

Frannie's mood changed again then, her spirits soaring with the aircraft. Three moods in ten minutes: sexual excitement, nervous apprehension and now the relief of delight as she gazed through the window with the innocent rapture of a young teenager.

She glanced over her shoulder, her face wearing a big smile. 'Hey, Gregory, isn't that something?' she enthused. 'Isn't that beautiful out there?'

Gregory nodded stoically. 'Beautiful, yeah. Right.'

'You don't sound *terribly* enthusiastic.'

'I've probably seen it too many times before, Lady Ballington.' He nodded out of the window and managed to crack a smile. 'But you're right. It is pretty.'

'You have the air of a man who's seen it *all* before.' She stubbed out the half-smoked cigarette, noticing as she did so that the tight-sprung Matilda was beginning to uncoil somewhat, but knowing from experience that she would not be approachable for a while yet.

Gregory said, 'You can say that again. I've been around a fair old while.' And he had. From his late teens he'd seen army action, fought as a mercenary in various parts of the world and then been recruited by the crack British SAS; and he was now in his middle forties. But despite this, he doubted if he had ever seen, could not even remember ever even *hearing* about, a situation similar to the one he was headed into with the seductive young wife of Lord Ballington.

After a while, the novelty of the candy-floss landscape beginning to wear thin and Matilda sufficiently composed to be fixing them drinks, Frannie asked Gregory if he would like to watch a movie. Mischievously, as she offered him a small choice of the latest, preferred productions, she rounded the list off by saying, 'Or, if you prefer, I've got some great porno. Really horny stuff, the latest from California.'

Gregory treated himself to his maximum allowance, a lingering, sexually obvious look at Frannie's figure which was highlighted by a tight, cream fine satin Ungaro travelling suit which clung to her like skin. Then he tore his eyes away, sighing. 'If you don't mind, I think we'd better stick to Polanski. My lady?' he said.

# 2
# New York, New York

On her first morning in a surprisingly clear-skied New York, the city playing host to an early spring, Frannie went on a spending spree. After Bond Street in London her favourite places to shop were Fifth and Madison Avenues and by lunchtime she had managed to spend over fifty thousand dollars, exhausting Gregory who trailed along with her through store after store in the process.

The Big Apple being a city with sex very much on its mind it appropriately offers, most especially through the Sonia Pykiel and Emanuel Ungaro boutiques on Madison belonging to Bonni Keller who regularly scours the lingerie ateliers of Europe for her magnificent collection, a selection of female undergarments as stunning and varied as can be found in any city in the world, Paris included. In buoyant mood, Frannie indulged herself to the full, frequently teasing Gregory by holding various skimpy, sensuous items against herself and innocently soliciting his opinion.

But, that afternoon, relaxing in the luxury flat which Lord Ballington kept on Park Avenue, a magnificent penthouse sixty-five stories above Central Park, Frannie found that she was apprehensive, little doubts about the course on which she was about to embark nagging at her. She kept wishing that Victor was there with her, that Victor, as always in the past, would steer them into sexual adventure; the prospect of taking her first step alone in that direction was pretty close to daunting. She realized that she had been leafing through the copy of *Vogue* in her hands without reading the words or even seeing the pictures and, laying it aside on a lapis-lazuli-topped table she got to her feet and crossed to a window. There she stood statue-still, her eyes on the breathtaking panorama of New York City but her entire mind hung on the thought that somewhere down there was an unknown he, or she, or indeed a them, with whom, if all went as it was planned to, she would be having sex in just a few hours' time. After long moments the statue unfroze and Frannie smiled at her touch of nerves, the tiny dimple, of which Lord Ballington was so fond, indenting itself briefly by the side of her mouth. She turned from the window, and decided that a Jacuzzi would be just the thing to help her relax.

Frannie's bathroom was a study in luxury, not simply a utility room, but a room in which to luxuriate. The walls and ceiling were lined with a rich redwood; the sanitary fittings were in the palest of pink and were imported from Italy and incorporated solid silver taps and levers and hand-painted museum-design porcelain fixtures. There was a sauna for four, a Jacuzzi for six, a round sunken bathtub and two showers with fine-touch temperature controls. In one corner stood an exercise unit with a massage table, an exercise mat and a ballet barre; in another, where it could be viewed comfortably from the bathtub or Jacuzzi, was a large TV screen and a video unit. Unobtrusive speakers produced superb quadrophonic sound, a subtle arrangement of tinted mirrors allowed a person to see themselves simultaneously from any angle, and the lighting could be changed to suit the mood from a keyboard of electronic controls, placed within reach of both tub and Jacuzzi, and incorporating controls for sound and television and even the lock on the door.

There was a well-stocked bar and fridge and bare feet were spoiled by a wall-to-wall carpet of the softest wool. To soften any possible harshness of line, lush houseplants grew and trailed all around the room.

Frannie punched two keys; the outside world was shut out as shades slid quietly closed over two picture windows and the room was filled with a soft, reddish-green glow from hidden lighting. She selected a Lionel Richie tape and, as the Jacuzzi began to fill, she stripped off her clothes, leaving them scattered on the floor. Naked, she stepped close to one of the figure-length mirrors and switched on the small white spotlight above it to study her reflection. Her body was as near to the present day's ideal of perfection as the female form could be: unblemished skin lightly tanned all over, her legs long, firm and slender, buttocks and stomach tight with no suggestion of excess fat, breasts just that fraction below large to be superb, the corona of the nipples a delicate pink, the whole vision framed by shiny, cascading blonde hair. At her crotch the subtle pubic mound was topped by a fuzz of light brown hair, soft to the touch, soft on the eye, amazingly conveying the impression of innocence begging to be lost. Her eyes moved across her other images living in other mirrors and reflected in the glass before her, a woman completely feminine from any angle, and she was pleased, but in an ingenuous, not a narcissistic, way.

She ran a hand through her hair then moved to the Jacuzzi, added a blue foaming gel to the water and stepped in. Closing the taps she pressed buttons to activate the jet streams, then closed her eyes as warm water began to pound her body, giving her the impression of three pairs of hands massaging her at once.

Ten minutes of this was always enough; any more she found tiring. After switching off the power unit she rang for Matilda who appeared within seconds, not quite dowdy. She had retouched her greying hair and made an effort with make-up, but, the bi-focals still gave her four eyes which stared down at her naked mistress, buried up to the chin in blue foam. Frannie patted the marble ledge which framed the Jacuzzi. 'Why don't you park yourself?' she said. 'I feel like a little talk.'

Matilda obliged. 'What about, Frannie?' Her accent, her casual use of her mistress's christian name, betrayed her origins. Matilda, Lady Ballington's personal maid, was to the manor born.

Frannie shrugged. 'Anything. I simply didn't feel like being on my own any more.'

With the noise of the air and water jets pulsing through the water stilled, the haunting sounds of Lionel Richie singing 'Hello' sounded louder in the room. 'You like the music?'

'You know I adore him.'

'Oh, I forgot. Let's talk about you. You know, I was thinking a little while ago, you really must conquer your absurd fear of flying. We're going to be travelling a great deal in the next few weeks and I hate to see you getting upset.'

'I can't help it. I try to. The safest form of transport and all that, I tell myself. But being logical doesn't help. My stomach gets in a dreadful, messy knot and I perspire.' She shrugged. 'But you don't have to worry about me. Once I'm up I'm all right, and I won't die from it.'

Frannie laughed. 'No you won't. Not unless we all do.' She paused, staring hard at Matilda. 'Tell me something frankly. Don't you ever find it kind of curious, annoying perhaps, this sort of role reversal of ours?'

'Not really. Well, perhaps, just on the odd occasion. Probably when I drink a touch more than usual.'

'Which is very seldom. Mind you, when it happens you *do* tie one on, Matilda.'

Matilda grinned. 'Don't I? But as you say, very seldom. Seriously, most of the time I find my life with you and Victor quite satisfactory.' Then she smiled insinuatingly, shifting her gaze from Frannie's face to where her body lay hidden beneath the foam, those four eyes seeming to bore right through it. 'Sometimes it's much *more* than satisfactory.'

'Yes.' Frannie lifted a sudsy arm and trailed a wet finger tip along the edge of the tub, her hand coming to rest lightly on Matilda's upper thigh. 'That aside, it's a funny situation. In a way, *you* should be the one with a maid, not me.'

'I suppose so. But then a skint upper class is the way of the world today. Impoverished nobility and all that. But you both treat me as more or less part of the family.'

Frannie put pressure on Matilda's thigh. 'In more ways than one.'

'Quite.'

She squeezed again, then took her hand away. 'Why don't you fix us a drink? Open some champagne and we'll toast New York.'

Whilst Matilda was ministering with patent inexpertise to the cork of a bottle of Dom Perignon, Frannie remarked, 'You know, I can't help envying you your bloodline, if not your lack of money. I wish I'd had your upbringing instead of being just plain middle class.' She grimaced. '*Lower* middle class at that.'

Matilda wrenched awkwardly at the cork then rammed her thumbs under its lip and with a sudden pop it came free, sailed across the room, bounced off the wall and fell into the tub whilst the agitated champagne foamed out onto the carpet in a thick stream.

Frannie laughed. 'Hey, there's no need to shoot me. There's not a class war going on here!'

'Champagne corks versus brown ale tops,' Matilda

24

said. Then she muttered, 'Wasted half the damn bottle, sorry.' She put two glasses on the marble and half-filled them. 'Thinking about it,' she said, 'You've adapted to your station perfectly. Wife to one of the richest men in England, a lady. I mean, nobody could know that you weren't born to it.'

'Thanks.' Frannie took a sip of champagne then stared reflectively at Matilda over the rim of her glass. 'There's something I've never quite understood about you. You're a highly intelligent woman, you had a wonderful education. How come you never set out on some sort of a career?'

'It was the wonderful education which blew the last of father's savings. And, despite that, the thought of a career was always somewhat odious to me. There was a time when I did hope to marry into my class, but, no Mister Right. So,' she shrugged, raising her glass to the megabathroom, 'This is the next best thing. I live in the surroundings which I crave. They're all around me.' She paused. 'Cheers.'

'Sure.' Frannie eased herself up out of the water, suds slipping gently down glistening flesh. 'Would you like to dry me?'

'What do you think?' Matilda placed her glass carefully on the tub edge while her eyes feasted on Frannie's body.

'I think so, yes.'

Matilda fetched a big pink towel, the material soft as lambswool, and draped it over Frannie's shoulders from where it hung to below her knees. She began to move her hands slowly and firmly over Frannie's body, caressing as much as drying her mistress's fine body, the hands side by side, insistent, arousing, lingering long after they were dry at her breasts, at her buttocks, high up on her inner thighs. Frannie lay with her head back, her eyes closed, the eternal hedonist being pampered in her sybaritic bathroom. Folding the towel away from Frannie and exposing her naked body, letting the towel slide slowly down her back, Matilda dropped to her knees, her hands behind Frannie's buttocks, grasping them with a sudden greed as her tongue flicked out and tasted her little nub of a clitoris, bringing a quick gasp to her lips.

Lady Ballington pushed Matilda's head away and wriggled from her grasp. 'Not yet,' she said, quietly, going to the bathroom door, opening it and turning to face Matilda as she got up from her knees. 'I want us to play a little game. I'm going to try on some of the lingerie I bought this morning and leave it for you to decide which set I shall wear tonight.'

'I want you, Fran.' Matilda's voice dropped half an octave.

'*After* you choose.' Frannie's head cocked naughtily to one side, her dimple puckering.

The first set was a watery yellow three-piece in organdie from Yves Saint Laurent, the panties skimpy, edged with fine white lace, the bra with holes for the nipples and a tight fitting mini-slip which was more lace than organdie. Frannie pirouetted in it, laughing delightedly. '*Tres* sexy, *n'est-ce pas*?'

Matilda said nothing, watching every move in rapt fascination as Frannie stripped naked again, poured herself into another set, then another, then yet another, her movements fluid and effortless, rivalling those of the most experienced of strippers. Finally she caught her breath as Frannie assembled on her body the pieces of an item from Bonni Keller: sheer white mousseline. Cami-knickers with the finest webwork of silken lace running down the sides and around the bottom, a delicate little bra made almost entirely of that same, silken lace and a garter belt to match. Breaking open a cellophane packet she let white silk stockings unfold and trail down her legs. 'With these to match,' she murmured. 'Pretty. *Very* pretty.'

'Stunning.' Matilda licked her lips. 'That's the one, Frannie. That you shall wear tonight. Put the stockings on.'

As Frannie rolled the stockings up her slender legs, clipping the tops into suspenders, Matilda went to her, taking off her glasses; without them her droopy, hazel eyes seemed strangely sensual in their myopia. 'That outfit is adorable,' she intoned. 'And so are you.' Putting her arms around Frannie, she clasped her buttocks with the same greed as in the bathroom, and kneaded them.

Aroused, to Frannie the hands were hot through the mousseline. She felt that familiar tightening at the back of her throat produced by the excitement which preceded sex. Voice husky, she said, 'You're quite sure? This, then, for my first sex scene in New York?'

'Second. After I've christened it.' And Matilda was back on her knees, sliding her hands behind Frannie's stockinged calves, whispering, 'Soft as skin,' then moving them up, above the stocking tops and bare thighs, slipping her chubby fingers under the lower edge of the cami-knickers, pulling Frannie tight to her and burying her face in the Bonnie Keller mousseline-cosseted crotch.

Feeling the heat and the damp as Matilda blew gently into the material, at the same time wetting it with her tongue, Frannie's knees gave slightly as she urged herself harder against Matilda's mouth, her hips wriggling, and moaned. Still breathing hotly into Frannie's crotch, Matilda carefully pulled her knickers down, moving her mouth away for a fraction to work them down to her thighs, then probed with her tongue, insistently, deeply inside her by now very wet mistress. The tongue substituted for two gentle fingers, working inside her, in out, in out, sliding easily in the juices as Matilda licked Frannie's clitoris, the fingers of the other hand deep in the cleft of her

27

buttocks, one of them teasing the little pink hole.

Feeling wickedly perverse – lesbianism was a practise which she had been encouraged to learn to enjoy by Lord Ballington, and was not a natural inclination – Frannie pushed Matilda's head away from her and looked down into sulky eyes which saw her face, even from that closely, as only a blur. With a catch in her voice she murmured, 'Take your knickers down, Matilda. Show me that beautiful cunt.'

Matilda poked the two wet fingers into her mouth, her head tilted back suggestively as she sucked off Frannie's juices. Then, getting to her feet, she stepped back, felt behind her for the bed and, finding it, laid down and pulled her black satin skirt high above her hips, splaying her legs and fingering herself through plain white cotton panties while Frannie insisted through tense lips, 'Let me *see* it.'

Quickly, then, Matilda stripped off her panties, leaving them hanging around one silver-chained ankle, and with her fingers spread herself wide for Frannie's lascivious stare. Frannie, as ever liking to talk about it, breathed, 'Yes, yes. Like that. Show me your cunt.' She stooped, sliding her hands under Matilda's ample arse and pulling her crotch up and into her face, smelling and tasting her aroused womanhood, pushing her tongue in as far as it would go, holding it there inside for long moments, taking it out, making it flicker, reptilian, around the tip of Matilda's aroused clit. After a while, she rolled aside, and took off the brand-new cami-knickers, their crotch wet with the mingling of her cunt juices and Matilda's saliva.

Matilda, lying with her eyes closed as Frannie undressed her, played urgently with herself. Then Frannie stood by the bed, watching her masturbate, marvelling at the plump, delectably smooth flesh, almost a Rubens, but no trace of pink, the skin marble white, the deep black thatch of pubic hair a startlingly erotic contrast. Fascinated by the sight, lust shining in her eyes which never left Matilda's body, she slipped out of her stockings and suspenders and the lacy bra and, naked, lay down beside Matilda on the bed, playing with the fat tits, sucking on the nipples as Matilda's fingers worked even faster.

Curiously, they had never kissed each other on the lips. It was an unspoken law between mistress and maid who had lustily enjoyed each other's bodies many times and in a wealth of erotic combinations. Rather like in the casual relationship between prostitute and client, that would have been an impropriety. Lord Ballington, screwing Matilda one afternoon at Stratton, largely to satisfy one of Frannie's voyeuristic moods, had once attempted to kiss her and was pushed away and rudely admonished for it.

'Let's do it,' Frannie muttered, changing positions as Matilda rolled onto her side, then, breasts tight against bellies, hands groping behind thighs and buttocks, fingers in buttock clefts teasing the tight little holes, they went hungrily to work on each other's cunts, inner thigh muscles and buttocks tensing and relaxing at briefer and briefer intervals as they approached their climaxes together, Frannie coming first with a tight little scream but continuing to pleasure Matilda, finishing her off moments later with two fingers working inside her like a cock and Matilda shouting her orgasm.

Long minutes of contented satiation followed, as they lay side-by-side on their backs, their eyes closed, heartbeats and breathing returning to normal, a gradual awareness of background music, eyes flickering open, smiling at one another, Frannie sitting, stooping over Matilda, kissing her on one nipple.

Then Frannie reached for a large patent leather handbag which sat on a bedside table, opened it up, saying lazily, 'Let's see if this contraption is as good as it's made out to be.'

Matilda frowned. 'What contraption?'

Frannie ignored the question. 'Why don't you run my bath?'

'Bath? But you've just had ...'

'A Jacuzzi,' Frannie finished for her. 'But now I feel sticky. Deliciously, I admit, but still ... And I want to be absolutely squeaky clean for later.' Fumbling inside the bag she brought out a video cassette. 'Besides, I thought we might want to watch this together, and what nicer place to do it than in a warm bath?'

'What is it?'

'You'll see.'

'Okay.' Matilda left the bed and disappeared through the bathroom door. There was a loud rushing sound as water poured, under strong pressure, through the tap. Frannie had time to enjoy three puffs from a Turkish cigarette before Matilda called out that the bath was ready.

Frannie activated the video equipment and inserted the cassette, rewinding it to its beginning, then settled in the round, steamy tub beside Matilda. The big TV screen flickered into life, there were some moments of static and then, the picture far from brightly lit, but nevertheless quite clear, the image of a maroon-covered double bed.

Matilda stared, finding the picture familiar but not quite placing it. 'What's *this*?'

'You'll see.' The video ran on for a while, but nothing seemed to be happening. There were undecipherable background noises, some music, but Frannie in any case had the sound low. Bits and pieces of female anatomy appeared from time to time indistinctly at one edge of the screen, that was all.

'It's hardly a major work of art, Frannie.' Matilda looked puzzled.

'Hang on.' Frannie climbed out of the tub and ran the tape fast forward. 'I must have spent more time

30

getting in and out of that lingerie than I realised.'

'Uh, uh. I think I'm seeing the light …'

'I thought you might. Here.' She stopped the tape, ran it back several frames, started it again and rejoined Matilda. 'Here it comes.'

A woman backed to the bed, reached behind her, and pulled her skirt high above her hips. Matilda gasped. 'That's *me*!'

Grinning, Frannie said, 'So it is. Well I'm damned – the thing actually worked! Marvel of modern science and all that.'

The on-screen Matilda was removing her panties now, then opening herself up while the off-screen version gaped. Then Frannie came into the picture, her blonde head diving down between Matilda's legs. Frannie exclaimed, a touch of incredulous delight in her voice, 'And that's *me*!'

Now that the figures on screen were close to the device installed in the handbag, the voices became more distinct. The two women could hear their sexual words and sounds from so short a time ago. Neither had seen themselves involved in sex on film before, and they began to find the experience extraordinarily erotic.

The end of the sequence found them locked in a passionate sexual embrace on the soft carpet directly beneath the TV screen.

Frannie was Fifth Avenue down to her Alain Harel shoes, the afternoon's selection of underwear hidden by a Diane Von Furstenberg three-piece ensemble in beige and paisley topped by a short white mink from Saks. She sat up front with Gregory in the white Mercedes 1000 as they headed, through fairly heavy traffic, for Harry Cook's exclusive club on West 57th Street. The indulgent afternoon had wound her right down but now, approaching the club which she had

31

patronised so many times with Victor, her nerves began to trouble her once again.

'Assuming you were a lady on her own,' she said to Gregory, 'and were going to a club with the, er, intention of getting picked up, where would you sit? At the bar or at a table?'

Gregory glanced sideways at her, clearing his throat, and raised an eyebrow. 'That's a pretty far-fetched assumption to start with,' he said. 'But given the required operation, I think I'd sit at the bar. Yes, the bar, no question about it.'

'Oh.' Frannie seemed surprised. 'Actually, I didn't expect you to voice much of an opinion.'

'I've been around a bit in my time, Lady Ballington. I 'ave indeed.'

'Yes.'

'Nervous, are you?'

'A touch.'

'To be expected, isn't it? Under the circumstances?' Having accepted this incredible, well-paid job with great gusto, and now that he was beginning to know Frannie a little, and to rather like her, Gregory was having reservations about her mission. But he left his little statement at that. It was none of his business to offer opinions, just to look after her back. 'Anyhow. At the bar,' he repeated. 'If it's, as you say, a strictly no-hookers place, I doubt if anyone's gonna try and give you a pull at a table.'

'Yes, I see. Thank you, Gregory.'

'Georgeous as you are,' He permitted himself, then treated her to one of his long, clothes-penetrating looks, unaware for several seconds that the impatient cacophony of horns from behind was aimed at him, sitting at a green light.

He found a parking space conveniently close to Cooks, escorted Frannie to the door, then returned to wait in the back seat of the Mercedes; it was no less comfortable than being at home – wide, chamois leather covered seats which he could stretch right across, a well-stocked bar, a small TV. He made himself a scotch and soda and settled back to watch *Dallas*.

Entrance at Cook's was strictly vetted, the door rigidly controlled by two men behind the desk which sat in a magnificent, though smallish, foyer with plinthed and fluted green marble columns. Frannie, instantly recognised, was treated with a politeness bordering on reverence, a hidden bell was pressed and Harry Cook himself, a dapper Englishman, appeared to greet her before a doorman had her coat off.

Cook had styled his club somewhat after the fashion of Annabelle's in London, and, like Annabelle's, it was a continuing success. Once inside, mingling with an on the whole youngish, almost boisterous crowd, Frannie began to relax. The overriding atmosphere was friendly, the place, with its old-world décor welcoming. There were two or three seats empty at the rather grand, highly polished mahogany bar, and Frannie picked one close to a corner, from where she had both a good view over the club and could study faces in the tinted glass mirrors which were backdrops for shelves of bottles and racks of gleaming glasses. It pleased her to hear one of the three barmen greet her with a cheerful, 'Say, Lady Ballington! Great to see you again.'

She remembered his name, too. She smiled. 'Hello. Thomas. Nice to be back.'

'Still the same tipple, is it? Smirnoff Vodka, tonic, no lemon?'

'That'll do very nicely. Thank you, Thomas.'

As he turned his back and began to mix the drink, he threw, over his shoulder, loudly so as to be heard above the music, 'Lord Ballington not with you?'

One or two heads had already turned at the sound

of a title, and she replied, unintentionally loud enough for all around her to hear, 'No, I'm on my own this trip. Lord Ballington's in England.'

As Thomas set her drink in front of her, a very young man next to her, perhaps twenty and with a boyish, heavily freckled face, said, 'Heh, excuse me, are you a *real* lady? I mean, for *real*?' And another young man with him grinned and broke in before Frannie could reply, 'Of course she's for real, are you *blind*? I never saw anything more like a lady in my life!'

Frannie laughed, amused by their ingenuity. 'Many thanks. I am, actually, married to a British Lord and that makes me a lady by *official* definition, yes.'

Freckle-face's friend addressed her. 'Yes, indeedy. But you sure don't need any official definition in my book.'

She chatted with them for some while and allowed them to buy her a drink, but then she found their company palled. They were pleasant enough, but really very young and surprisingly naïve for New Yorkers, and although men of their age could at certain times be a turn-on, she didn't particularly feel like steering this little encounter into sex. She found an excuse to break it off when she spied a woman she knew quite well, one of New York's cosmetic queens, Madeleine Mono, whom she secretly didn't much care for, as she fell into what Frannie thought of as the 'Jewish Princess' category. Escorted by a younger man, Madeleine seemed pleased to see her, and invited her to sit at their table.

This encounter proved to be the launching point for the evening. A little later on Madeleine's manfriend introduced her to a man whom she found instantly attractive and by eleven o'clock she was alone with him in an intimate little booth near the dance-floor.

His name was Paul. He was forty and his wavy hair was already grey with just a few dark streaks. He was tall, six foot two at least, and elegantly dressed. She particularly liked his almost thin face with its high, Slavic, cheekbones and his ready, slightly crooked smile; but his eyes faintly disturbed her, as he had a way of looking directly at her and then, at the wrong moment, darting furtive little glances around the room. He was from Boston, the owner of a book and magazine distributors, and was staying in New York for two nights on business. Like most Americans he was fascinated by her title and asked the usual amount of questions about the British nobility (I suppose you know Charles and Diana) but in an amusing, not an irritating fashion. He bought champagne and by the time they had downed half of the bottle they were holding hands across the table, impending sex more or less a tacit agreement.

He took her on the dance-floor then, but, fancying him as she did, she nevertheless decided there was something strange about the man. As they talked and danced, very close and slowly, she found their increasingly lengthy eye contact suggestive, but disturbing. He was possessed of the palest of grey eyes, a colour she did not recall having come across before and, each time they locked on hers the weirdest of feelings came over her; sex was in his look, but something more, something somehow a little twisted.

Their first kiss, swaying together in the middle of the floor, surrounded by smooching couples, warm bodies pressed together in almost a tribal mass, was long drawn out, their tongues instantly mingling, he pressing himself into her as he went rigid.

That first sexual contact sent a thrill wave down her spine and if he found her instant willing response surprising he didn't let it show. Paul whispered, drawing the words out and finishing them by blowing softly in her ear, 'You're some horny chick, your ladyship.'

35

Once again, in those eyes, she found something not quite right. It could even have been amused contempt. But she smiled and said, 'Just healthy.'

His next words shook her. The timing, for one, was all wrong, at least in her sexual look. 'You like to talk dirty?'

She kept her expression neutral. 'What kind of a question is that?'

'My kind of a question. Why don't you answer me?' he paused, moving his lower body against her. 'You feel me, don't you?' She could hardly not. His cock was hard against her abdomen and, despite her conflicting mental impressions she was responding physically, getting wet between her legs.

'Of course I feel you. That's one thing – words are another.'

'Sure they are. And the right combination can be dynamite.' He paused. 'Do you like to talk dirty, Lady Ballington?'

She sighed. 'Okay. Sometimes,' she admitted. 'But it depends who and where. And when.'

'Now, not?'

'I don't know.' She didn't. And yet … the conversation was beginning to contribute to her wetness.

'You want *me* to talk dirty with *you*, *now*?'

She stared at him. 'It seems that you already are.'

His hands left the small of her back and travelled down to her bottom. He said, his voice at its normal level. 'I'm going to give you the fucking of your life.'

Frannie swallowed. 'Oh,' she said, weakly.

'I think you need my prick in you, Lady B.' His strong hands squeezed her arse. 'What do you think?'

Frannie took long moments to answer, but when she did she could not help what she said. 'I think so too.'

'I'm going to show you one of the biggest cocks you've ever seen. Come on.' He danced her off the floor and right up to their table. Frannie guessed he was trying to hide his erection, at the same time wondered why he should bother after the way he had been talking.

As they sat down Frannie tried to relieve her tension with laughter, but it did not come out right. She said, awkwardly. 'Well, you, er, certainly have a winning way with words.'

He topped up her glass, raising an eyebrow and cocking his head, then looking her up and down. 'Somehow I don't think you really mind.'

'Maybe.'

'My place, then?'

'Where's that?'

'Bit of a dump. But it's all *we* need. I'm staying at a pal's. He's not from New York either but he keeps a small pad downtown.'

'I've got a place in Park Avenue. We can go there if you like.'

'Luxury?'

'Rather.'

'Yeah, well. I tell you what. We go downtown. It's going to be a lot more fun.'

'Why?'

'You'll see when we get there.' Those eyes again. Not quite right. Kinky, was that the word for it?

Frannie shivered slightly. 'I'm not sure if I like the sound of that.'

'Will you trust me? – You're going to like the feel of it, that's a promise.' He stood. 'I'll be right with you. I'm going to pick up the tab and make one quick call.'

She went to the ladies where she fixed her appearance, which did not need it, but failed to straighten up her nerves, which did. She found herself extremely apprehensive about going off God-knew-where with Paul, almost wanting to chuck the idea, to slip away, but sexual curiosity finally took her back to the table where he was waiting.

'I've ordered us a cab,' he said.

'Oh. You needn't have bothered. I have my car outside.'

'Fine.' But when they reached the Mercedes and he saw Gregory dozing in the back with the TV still on, he said, 'Hey, what gives? This is your car, with a man in it? What's the big idea?'

Tapping on the window, Frannie said, 'That's not a man. That's Gregory, my, er, chauffeur.'

Gregory, awake on the first rap, got out of the car and held the door open for them. Climbing in after Frannie, watching her legs, Paul said, 'You Brits do yourselves proud.'

'Uh-huh.'

As Gregory closed the driver's door, Paul said, leaning forward. 'You know your way to the Bronx?'

'The *Bronx*?' echoed Frannie.

'Don't give it a thought. It's just on the outskirts. Still quite a respectable neighbourhood.'

'You'll have to direct me, sir,' said Gregory.

'Still quite respectable' turned out to be a dreary, treeless road with very few streetlights, lined with ugly, turn of the century terraced houses in urgent need of facelifts but looking sad rather than ominous. They drew up outside a number fifty-two, three stories of grubby granite, peeling brown paintwork, one of the ground floor windows cracked and patched up with tape and Paul, his hand under Frannie's dress, whispered in her ear, 'This is it. This is where you get to handle the biggest prick you've ever seen. Like I promised.'

As Gregory opened the door for them, Frannie suddenly dreaded going into that awful house with this strange man and his dirty talk, yet her sexual curiosity was such that the dread was almost a part of

38

the lure of the package. Swivelling out of the car she fingered her emerald ring; at least she need not feel unsafe. If anything bad happened she had her prearranged set of electronic signals to Gregory.

Paul, opening a tired, creaky door, said, 'That guy stays around for as long as you want?'

'All night, if necessary. That's what he's paid for.'

Then they were climbing faded, linoleum-covered stairs in the dim light thrown by one, unadorned light bulb, through a faintly unpleasant, sweetish smell which Frannie failed to identify and Paul was saying, 'I'm sorry, it's a dump, like I told you. But it's okay inside. Listen.' He stopped by a door, turning her to face him and holding her by the elbows, giving her another of his weird looks. Then he touched her between her legs, pressing his fingers into the material. 'You *are* as switched on as I think you are? Right?'

Funny question, doing nothing to relieve apprehension. '*Why*, for God's sake?'

He rang the bell. *Rang the bell*? Frannie's heart missed a beat. Then he said, 'It's just that I arranged a special surprise for you. You'll like it, for sure, but I want you to be prepared for a *very* special surprise on the other side of that door.'

Frannie, not quite scared, stared in awed fascination at the door as there was the sound of bolts sliding back, a chain lifted, and finally the creaking of a handle. The door swung open to reveal, bathed in bright light, the figure of a naked man whose flaccid penis, hanging between muscular, hairy thighs, must have been at least eight inches long. Smiling, he said, 'Welcome, friends!'

A totally stunned Frannie, her eyes rivetted on that mammoth tool, heard Paul say, 'Get the surprise? The biggest prick you've ever seen. Not mine, his. Meet

39

Stanley. Stanley this is the sensation I told you about on the phone. Lady Frannie Ballington.' He draped an arm across Frannie's immobile shoulder. 'Well, are we going in?'

# 3
# It Takes Two, Baby

Frannie's feet refused to budge. Of naked men she had
seen and enjoyed plenty, but they had always been
dressed, in some way or other, at the outset. And Paul
was right, she had never set eyes on such a penis. The
freaky surprise, this nude stranger with his massive
cock, sent her into a momentary state of shock. She
was vaguely aware of Paul's arm insisting her forward,
and that the naked man had a not unpleasant face and
a perfectly friendly smile, and she heard Paul saying,
'Come on, Frannie, are we going to stay here all night?'
with unmistakeable amusement in his voice, but still
she did not move.

The other man, Stanley, had moved aside to let them
pass. There were moments when she almost turned
and ran, then the shock subsided and, touching her
ring, taking comfort in the thought that she had a
secret alarm system should anything sinister arise, she
allowed herself to be shepherded into the apartment.

It was a high-ceilinged, spacious, studio apartment
with elaborate cornice work running around the walls
and over the floor-to-ceiling bay windows. Functional,
just lacking the warmth of a home, it was, as Paul had
said, quite all right, clean, smelling of fresh paint.
Colourful, framed Paul Klee prints were spaced rather
too evenly around the white walls, not quite doing
enough for them; there were single beds in the two
corners across from the windows, neatly made and

scattered with cushions, some crammed bookshelves, a bar, a colourless G-plan table with four chairs, a large leather bean-bag, one rather tired-looking sofa and a coffee table spread with magazines. A red-lacquered console contained hi-fi, television and video equipment and over the polished wooden floorboards were a number of soft-looking, pastel throw-rugs and one zebra skin. There was an absence of plants or flowers. All of which was but vaguely noticed by Frannie as she found herself being led to the sofa and heard the noise of the bolts to the door being shot back into place.

Gently, Paul encouraged her to sit. Then, propping himself on the edge of the dining table, hands behind him, wearing a frank smile under those disturbing eyes of his, he said, 'Relax, Frannie. We're going to give you a good time.'

For the moment, no words came to her. Frannie slowly stared in shocked fascination as Stanley turned his back on the door and crossed the room, his penis swinging. He said, completely at ease, 'Drinks then. What'll you have, Frannie?'

Frannie found her voice, but she spoke very deliberately, avoiding the threatened tremble. 'I think … a whisky. A *scotch* whisky, if you have it. Uh, some ice and just a dash of soda.'

Stanley grinned. He looked almost schoolboyish despite the fact that he was in his early thirties and losing his hair. 'What do you know?' he said. 'I do. I have it. One hefty scotch coming up. I'll join you, Paul? The usual?' The way he spoke, his movements, he may just as well have been clothed for all the concern his nakedness caused him.

Paul said, 'Fine.' Then he sat next to Frannie on the sofa, taking hold of her hand. 'You okay?'

Was she *okay*? Frannie glanced around the room, her surroundings for the first time beginning to swim into focus. A small moment of near-panic. Just what the hell was she *doing* here? She noticed that Stanley had tight, well-shaped buttocks. She liked a good rear end on a man. Was she okay? Probably. Just. Eyes once again on the dangling cock as Stanley fetched the drinks. She noticed that his faded tan was all over.

Finding an almost natural voice as she accepted her whisky she asked, 'Do you always open your door like that?'

'Not generally, no. Paul's idea. He's an evil bastard at times.'

'What evil?' Paul protested. 'It was a special surprise for my lady here.'

'Oh, it's that all right.' Frannie took a long, comforting slug from her glass, the ice tinkling. Then she spluttered. 'It certainly is.'

'It was supposed to be a big turn-on,' said Stanley.

'Really?'

'Is it turning you on?' Paul asked, squeezing her hand.

'No comment.' Very firmly. But there Stanley still stood, his formidable sexual equipment but three feet from her face and she tried not to look but her eyes kept coming back to it. The whisky-glow spread through her; she had some more.

'Good old scotch whisky,' said Stanley. 'Can't think why we Americans bothered to invent bourbon.'

It dawned on Frannie that she was all right, she was relaxing. These men were no threat to her, they wanted to have fun with her, sure, but nothing harmful. Well, especially this nude Stanley – Paul's eyes were sure to continue to trouble her. But she was beginning to realize that that was to do with the thoughts behind them; he evidently liked to manoeuvre people into kinky scenes, preferring them from the outset to a normal relationship, and his eyes suggested what his brain planned.

Paul stood. 'Let's get some atmosphere going

around here,' he said, and went to the console. 'What music sets your mood, Frannie?'

She dared. 'Whatever turns you on.'

'I like it.'

Stanley perched on the arm of the sofa, his legs carelessly apart, cock and balls still clearly on display, hanging against the yellow worsted covered arm. Frannie tried not to look.

'Rod Stewart, then,' said Paul, startling her. No way he could have known, but for her the gutsy music of Rod Stewart *was* sex. She occasionally played him when she felt like masturbating.

'Lighting effects are somewhat primitive,' Paul was saying as he switched off an overhead light and the wall lights, leaving on a solitary standard lamp. He disappeared through a door, returning with a bath towel which he draped over the shade. 'How's that?'

Frannie found the soft glow agreeable, anticipating sex, eager almost now, licking her lips. 'Splendid.' Voice turning husky. She drained her glass. 'Could I have another drink?'

'Sure.' Strains of vintage Stewart, 'Never a Dull Moment', as Stanley got her refill and stood directly in front of her again as he handed it to her, deliberately closer than before, his cock no more than a foot from her face.

Suddenly aware she was still wearing her mink, she began to shrug out of it. Moving behind her, Paul put his hands on her shoulders. 'No. Keep it on.'

She caught her breath. 'All right. Whatever you say.' Taking a longish, slow drink of whisky, eyes over the rim of the glass on the male organ suspended in front of her, she said, 'What happens next?'

Leaning forward, his lips brushing her ear, Paul whispered, 'Why don't you take that thing in your mouth, for starters?'

Very carefully, lips pursed, she placed the glass on

44

the floor. 'Okay.' She reached for Stanley with one hand, testing the weight of his balls with her slender fingertips then bent from the waist, poked her tongue between closed lips and trailed it from the tip of Stanley's uncircumcised monster into its root buried deep in dark pubic hair and slowly back down again, feeling it begin to stir as, using her other hand, and her tongue, she took three fat inches of it into the warmth of her mouth, looking up into slitting blue eyes as he muttered, 'Yeahhh,' and moved against her, his cock growing fast as she drew on it, her wet tongue teasing the head. Paul, licking inside her ear, searching hands sliding into the mink, down the wide blouse-neck and under her bra, thumbs and fingers finding her nipples, pinching.

Frannie, never thrown so dramatically, or quickly – ten minutes! – into sex with a total stranger before nor ever, apart from Matilda, taking part in a sex scene without the presence of Lord Ballington, was falling into this threesome with a lusty, crotch-wetting anticipation as Stanley's cock grew to its full splendour in her mouth. She wanted to be dirty. Very, *very* dirty.

Stanley's hard-on was immense. Making a fist around it, Frannie removed it from her mouth, consumed with horny fascination at it as she jerked her fist in quick little movements.

Pinching her nipples harder, not quite hurting her but making her back go rigid and bringing a soft gasp to her lips, Paul said, 'Was I right? Some tool, no?'

Fellatio being a practise she was addicted to, a penis in her mouth a pleasure to her as great, but in a much different way, as one inside her, Frannie mumbled something incoherent and closed her lips around Stanley's cock once more, began moving her head steadily back and forth, taking as much as she could in at each stroke, his pleasure grunts arousing her to greater efforts as she masturbated him at the same

45

time with thumb and index finger, her other hand toying with his balls.

Paul, releasing her tits, moved around the sofa, and dropped to his knees beside Stanley as she continued her greedy cocksucking, Paul's hands up her skirt, right up, all the way to the waist of those cami-knickers, hooking his fingers under the elastic, Frannie's hand leaving Stanley's balls to support herself as she helped Paul by slightly raising her bottom.

Taking the knickers to mid-thigh, then feeling for her cunt, probing it with two fingers, Paul murmured, 'Ready for that prick in you?' and Frannie made a low, excited sound which meant a very definite 'yes'.

Paul left her, and hauled the bean-bag over. 'Over this then. On your knees over this and pull your dress up. But *very* slowly.' This was said in a tone which brooked no resistance.

Frannie, awkwardly leaving the sofa for the bean-bag, knelt on the zebra rug and, behind her, fumbled for her dress, the two men standing back, intent, one mother-naked, the other fully dressed, three-piece suit and tie, bulging but unopened trousers. Trying to do it as she imagined Paul wanted, thinking, 'What a beautifully, dirty mind the bastard has', She worked the Diane Von Furstenberg paisley chiffon slowly, tantalisingly slowly, up her silk-covered thighs, over the half-mast panties, above stocking-tops and finally exposing the beautifully rounded buttocks and a nest of damp pubic hair, the dress coming to rest in an unruly pile with the mink in the middle of her back.

Rod Stewart's 'Mama, You've Been on my Mind', drowned the guttural sounds of male lust. Stanley wanked slowly; Paul did not, but his cold grey eyes invaded Frannie's parts. Frannie looked over her shoulder, but Paul forbad it. 'No, don't look around.'

46

So she stared forward, at the orange curtains over bay windows, feeling dreadfully exposed, longing to feel that massive cock in her, long, long moments passing as the men made her wait. Christ did they *know* what they were doing to her? Of course they did, they were doing it to themselves, too. Rod Stewart began another song: 'Angel'. She sensed Stanley closing in on her, and heard Paul saying, 'Open yourself. Wide.'

Hands behind her once more, breasts flattening into the bean-bag, fingers spreading herself, more waiting, like that, more naked than naked. Why doesn't the sod *fuck* me? Finally, a real, desperate *need*, a pleading, 'Fuck me, please, please, *please* fuck me!' That's what they were waiting to hear and oh, oh, oh, *oh*, out loud as the full length of Stanley's cock slid into her with one powerful thrust, lingering, throbbing, filling her as never before, starting to move, good, strong, steady *thrusts*, balls slapping noisily against the bean-bag, hands sliding beneath her, pulling aside the mink, gripping her breasts through chiffon. Frannie climaxing with a wail, Stanley pounding on as Paul stands in front of her, sliding his zipper down, muttering, 'A gorgeous, expensive lady being thoroughly fucked on her knees with all her clothes on. There is no sight in the world to be compared.'

Paul takes his cock out – a good one too, a good average, good and hard, going down on his knees, the trouser belt still fastened, masturbating fast in front of her eyes as Stanley brings Frannie on her way to another orgasm. Paul's cock in her mouth now, a cock at both ends, two pleasures combined, for most women a fantasy, for few a reality, for Frannie one of her favourite indulgences.

Stanley came noisily and at length, his cum flooding into her, his cock pulsating, out of control. And then Paul, unexpectedly, his cock only having been exposed and in her mouth for a mere minute or so, his sperm hitting the back of her throat. Swallowing it down, drinking it, loving the familiar, salty taste of it, climaxing again herself, her cries stifled by cock, Stanley still inside her too, slackening, his cum oozing out of her, trickling down her thighs.

Frannie, wanting more, much more, lay back on the sofa where they stripped her naked. Paul got out of his clothes then, his elaborately orchestrated opening scene over and a success. And they had another drink, Frannie wonderfully light-headed, hot between her legs, feeling good, *very* good. Paul switched the music to Sinatra, busied himself pushing one bed up against the other then, like Stanley earlier, he stood in front of, and deliberately close to, the seated Frannie, his sex organs at her eye level, nowhere near the size of Stanley, but very male. He said, 'You ever been in a sandwich, Lady B?'

She licked her lips, looking up at him from under lowered lashes. 'Uh, huh,' she said. 'You mean two men at once? One normally, the other in my rear end?'

'Not quite. I mean a proper sandwich. I'm no arse man and Stanley would split you in two.'

She glanced from Paul to Stanley, cock to cock. 'I'm intrigued.'

'A *real* sandwich, in my book, is two pieces of meat in the same roll. What you describe is two pieces of meat in separate rolls – if you get my drift.' He paused, 'What I'm talking about is two cocks in the same cunt.'

She let her eyes travel slowly up his lean torso, over the muscular chest with its mat of greying hair. 'I don't believe I've had the pleasure.'

'You're going to *love* it, Frannie.'

'Oh.' Weakly. Another slug of scotch. Then Paul was spread-eagling his legs over her thighs, kneeling on the sofa, pushing his genitals into her face, then rolling his cock against her cheek with one hand, releasing it. 'Get it up, Lady Ballington.'

No sweat. A limp cock in Frannie's sweet mouth could never be that way for long. Stanley joined them, kneeling beside her, then she was busily mouthing the two of them, first one, then the other, sucking them, tonguing them, coaxing them both into swollen hard-ons, tongue tip searching the tiny holes, green nailed fingers grasping the shafts, tossing them off a bit, a prick in either hand, then the glans of each together between her lips, doubling the pleasure.

Paul stood up and took her hand, pulling her up, leading her across the room. Stanley followed, both cocks pointing the way to the beds. Being laid down on her side, by Stanley, facing him, belly to belly, wet again, soaked, her thigh lifted over his, then the length of his massive cock invading her again, making her shudder. Paul, behind her, his chest tight against her back, digging a finger into her arsehole then finding, from behind, room next to Stanley's cock for his finger, then the head of his cock, easing the whole thing in there, tight against Stanley's, her vagina walls stretched, stretched, no pain, a feeling of being thoroughly *stuffed*. Incredible sensations, waves, the two cocks moving, one against the other, one up, the other down, one up, one down, regular, finding a rhythm, she quite still between the thrusting men, giddy with the feelings flooding her body from her cunt. She thought she had had everything, now *this*. And what about them, those two men inside her, were their cocks giving each other pleasure, as well as her and themselves as their rhythm steadily increased, flesh against flesh against flesh? Of course, they *must* be pleasuring each other, she knew it, but she didn't *care* what kind of kink she was involved with here, let them *do* it, for fuck's sake let them *do* it. Forever. Don't let it ever stop, ram those beautiful pricks up me, split my cunt wide open. *Do* it for Christ's sake, *do* me. Fuck me to *death*. Rambling aloud, not realizing it in her total physical abandon, voicing her excitement, bringing the men to yet higher peaks, with her words.

Slowing it down for a while, holding back, luxuriating in the sensations which coursed through their bodies, then speeding right up, going over the top, *slamming* into her, starting to crush her, Frannie uncaring, *crush* me. Final, violent, involuntary heaves, animal grunts, cum gushing into her from two cocks she, amazingly, coming right along with them, Paul stifling a wail from Frannie which, allowed to continue, could have brought the police, Stanley pulling out of her and spraying the last spurt of his sperm over her sweating belly.

They took her in turns after that, exhausting themselves on her. When she got dressed at five-fifteen, they were both heavily asleep and she, having napped for perhaps half an hour, felt curiously refreshed. But she wanted still more of these two horny bastards. She was thoroughly launched into her adventures now, the nervous part behind her, and she intended to get every bit as much as she could out of each situation. Before slipping away she left a note, insisting that both men come to Park Avenue for dinner the following evening.

Gregory, waking even before she rapped on the car window, his combat-alertness ever fine, let her in, saying, before getting himself into the driver's seat, 'Pleasant evenin', was it?'

Frannie smiled an arch smile. 'I'll say.'

As he drove them homewards, Gregory marvelled at how fresh Lady Ballington looked, how bright were her eyes. Been up to hardly anything at all, he said to himself, happy with that idea.

Frannie was a good cook, she enjoyed it, and when she dined at home, which was seldom, she liked to prepare the meal with her own hands, with Matilda naturally doing all the dirty work and serving table, though when Frannie and Victor dined alone, or with family or close friends she was generally invited to join them. On this occasion, she was not, which, she did not mind in the least, but she treated Frannie's guests to many searching glances as she to'ed and fro'ed to the table, deciding that the balding one was quite all right but that the older one had something distinctly odd ball about him, especially around the eyes.

Frannie had prepared a simple meal – gaspacho followed by lobster served with a French dressing and rounded off with rum baba. The conversation was inconsequential but enjoyable. Stanley, who turned out to be a moderately successful advertising executive, was particularly amusing. She commented on his total lack of concern about opening the door nude the previous evening and he told her that he was used to being that way in front of people; he spent time in nudist camps, and when she said that there surely was a *difference*, that opening the door of one's flat naked to a complete stranger was hardly the same as flouncing around with a lot of other nude people, he grinned wickedly and said, not a lot, but the thrill of exhibitionism was somehow lacking at a nudist camp.

Over coffee she confided to them her plans for a round-the-world sexual adventure for once shaking their American seen-everything, men-of-the-world attitude. But she failed to mention the recording equipment. She had not had it with her the previous evening, her confidence in what she was doing unestablished, but tonight she felt right about it; *tonight* she intended to film.

Stanley said, 'You're some extraordinary lady, Frannie. It takes guts to set out on something like that. You could get yourself into serious trouble.'

Then she told them about Gregory and the electronic warning system. Paul grunted. 'I thought there was more to that guy than met the eye.' He finished his coffee. 'A delightful meal, my love. I suppose we should be honoured. Stage one in the Honourable Lady Ballington's sexual package tour.'

She poked her tongue out at them, provocatively, a deliberate, lewd look. 'Not so bad a beginning.'

Stanley said, 'Glad you think so,' and added, 'I always heard the British aristocracy was a decadent breed, but this takes the cake!'

'My dear man, of *course* we're decadent – we invented it.' Matilda appeared and began clearing away the cups. 'Aren't we, Matilda?'

Matilda stopped in her tracks and frowned. 'Aren't we what?'

'Decadent. We British upper classes.'

'Not half. Of *course* we are, darling.'

'There you are, you see. Matilda should know; her very distinguished family tree stretches back to Henry the Eighth.'

Amused, Paul shook his head, refraining to comment on a mistress – servant relationship which was totally beyond his understanding. The British, he decided right then, were all a little nuts. As Matilda departed he said, 'So, a sexual journey. I'm afraid you'll find that there's not much new in the world. Everything's been done before.'

Frannie objected. 'Not to *me* it hasn't.' She tilted her head meaningfully. 'Take last night ...'

'Sandwich.'

'Something of the fashion.'

'You want more of that treatment tonight?'

'Yes?' Her throat constricted.

Stanley said slowly, '*Our* pleasure, your ladyship.'

She stared levelly at him. 'That as well. Obviously.'

Paul broke in. 'Say, I have a great idea for you. I'm in magazines, as you know. Got a friend down in Florida who produces a terrific porno magazine. *Prick*, it's

an acre, a great deal of it lawn bordered by cypress and dotted with fir trees, dogwood and flowering shrubs; there was also a rose garden and a huge ornamental pool well-stocked with colourful tropical fish. The surprise of all this was agreeable; for some reason her very English mind had associated the production of erotic material with a sleazy location, and here she found herself in the beautiful garden of a magnificent house, a stylish, established residence with black-timbered exterior walls and finely leaded windows.

'Lady Ballington?' Her name was spoken softly but the man's approach had been soundless on the soft turf and, startled, she opened her eyes. She saw a tall, heavy set man of about fifty with a good head of wavy, grey hair and dressed in a neat white suit, an open-necked black silk shirt with matching pocket handkerchief and gleaming black shoes. His generous smile exhibited perfect teeth, too white to be real, and he was offering his hand, which she took.

'Glad to have you here.' He smiled again. 'I'm David Hansom. We spoke on the telephone.'

Frannie's first impression of the man she found immensely reassuring; there was an easy, confident friendliness about him. Getting to her feet, she was still engaged in the handshake. 'Yes, we did,' she said. 'How do you do? I must say you have a rather splendid home here.'

'Thank you. Not bad, I think.' He broke his grip. 'Nice location, too. Away from the hustle and bustle of the coast, but close enough to be in constant contact. Very private.' He nodded towards the lake with its scattering of boats. 'We're actually four meters above sea level. Well, the lake is.'

'How fascinating.'

'Yes, well.' He stared at her, appraising her frankly. 'My God, but you're a beauty.'

She smiled delightedly. The man obviously meant

his words. 'Why, thank you.'

'You really are something else. Very special. You're quite sure you want to do this?'

'You mean nice girls don't?'

'On the contrary. They do. But ...' He shrugged. 'The Honourable Lady Ballington. A society beauty and then some ...' His words trailed off.

'Well, you know very well why I'm here. But I must warn you that I've never done anything like it before so of course I don't know how I'm going to feel. If you see what I mean.'

'Understood.' He paused. 'Forgive me the liberty, but from what Paul said about you I would think you're going to feel just fine, Lady Ballington.'

'Mmm.' She stared levelly at him. 'Well, we'll see. I hope so. You, um, you said on the phone that there might be more than just one man involved?'

'There might. But it's really up to you. I don't believe in getting people into situations where they feel uncomfortable. I'll tell you something, though, and this is a curious fact. Almost every woman who has approached me, and I've been in the business more than twenty years so that mounts up to a heck of a lot of females, has been eager to appear in some sort of group scene. I'm not talking so much about the girls I get from model agencies and acting schools, that sort of thing, that's a different situation. Just the ones who write direct, or come to me via friends, such as yourself.'

Frannie thought about it. 'You know, that doesn't entirely surprise me.'

'Then you're a woman of the world.'

'You might say that, yes.' She smiled a beguiling smile of virginal innocence.

'Sensational!'

'What?' she asked knowing full well what he was thinking.

'The smile, Lady Ballington. The smile. I'll *have* to capture that.'

'Oh. Well, I'll try. And please call me Frannie.'

'Fine. While we're discussing the subject I'll tell you something else which *may* surprise you, Frannie. Of all the women who write sending photographs, most ask to pose making love with two or more men. And it always turns out with the ones I use that afterwards they tell me how they'd dreamed of such a scene but, would you believe it, they'd been too inhibited to get it together for themselves. They saw writing to me as the only possibility of realizing their fantasies. I mean, like, it's never for the money, they're very happy to do it for nothing. I swear, some of them would even pay me!'

'But do you pay them anyway?'

'Of course. Matter of principle, and good sense. I'm going to pay you.'

Frannie laughed. 'I've never been paid for anything in my life.'

'There's always a first time.'

'Yes. And as a matter of fact I insist on it.' Wetting her lips, she glanced out over the vast lake and then quickly back to David Hansom, staring him straight in the eyes. 'I rather think it might add flavour to the adventure if I'm paid. An air of prostitution.'

'Ha hah! Now you begin to exhibit the female mind at its most wickedly devious.' He grinned. 'Obviously only the very top rates will persuade so gorgeous a lady to remove her clothes? And the et cetera.'

'Clearly. Especially the et cetera.' Frannie realized that she was beginning to enjoy herself.

'A drink?'

'Thanks. Something cool and refreshing. What do you suggest?'

'How about a Campari with soda?'

'Wonderful. With straws and a slice of lemon if you can manage.'

'Right. I'll join you.' He disappeared into the house but when he returned, moments later, he was carrying only a polaroid camera. 'Test shots,' he said. 'After the drink, that is. Why don't we sit down?'

They did, Frannie speculatively eyeing the camera in his lap. He said, 'I need to see how you photograph before I decide what story to set up.'

'I see.'

The Negro appeared bearing a butler's tray with its legs erect which he placed carefully on the lawn between them. Ice tinkled against the sides of two highball glasses. Hansom took one and raised it as Frannie picked up the other. 'Bottoms up. That's what you English say, isn't it?'

'Very appropriate.' Frannie half repressed a giggle. 'Under the circumstances.'

Hansom chuckled. 'Excellent. You have a sense of humour.'

'Do you think I'm going to need it?'

'Hardly. Perhaps on the odd occasion. But sex should never be funny.'

'No.'

They chatted frivolities as they sipped their Camparis, the idyllic picture of the successful American businessman and his society lady friend belying the reality of the pornographer and his model-to-be. After a while he removed the cover from his camera and got to his feet. It was the bulky Land model 355, the last of its kind before the kind of polaroid where the film shoots out the front and develops itself.

'Cumbersome, and slow,' he remarked. 'But it takes a far better picture than the latest ones.'

'What do you want me to do?'

'Just stay where you are for the minute.' He aimed the camera. 'Let's try that smile, shall we?'

The breeze had blown her hair forward and she

shook her head and brushed it back over her shoulders then tried 'that' smile. The camera clicked, a tinny sound in the quiet air and Hansom pulled the undeveloped picture cleanly out from the inside and deftly set the timer to sixty seconds. 'It's the hanging about I find so boring with these things,' he said. 'Funny how just one little minute drags when you're waiting for it to pass.'

She stirred the last inch of Campari and the almost melted ice with two straws. 'That smile didn't feel quite right. Bit like this impatient minute of yours in a way. The forced smile. They both impose on one.'

He raised an eyebrow. 'I have a philosopher on my hands as well as a beauty.'

'I wouldn't go so far as to say that!'

The timer stopped its whirring. Peeling off the backing paper, he studied the result. 'There.' Holding the damp print carefully between finger and thumb he showed it to her. 'Quite good. You're very photogenic. You never can tell until the moment of truth. The smile's not quite what I wanted but it demonstrates its potential. We'll get there.' He paused. 'On the day.'

Frannie experienced a fractional constricting of her throat. The day.

'Now the legs, huh? I want you to keep sitting there but pull your dress up as high as it will go. To your navel.' There was a moment's hesitation on Frannie's part. 'I mean, if you don't mind, that is.'

'All right.' And she took her skirt by its hem and bunched it up, holding it tight into her waist, exposing a lacy, white suspender belt and silk charmeuse cami-knickers. 'Like this?'

'Perfect.' The camera clicked again. 'Do you always wear such sensational underwear?'

She was beginning to feel coquettish, perversely still sat with her skirt at her waist though he was waiting for the picture to develop, 'Always.'

59

'Mmm.' He stared at her for several seconds, in the region of her mid-section, then he said. 'You can pull the dress down now.'

'Oh.' She did, in no hurry about it.

'You know, more than half the girls who come here to work have no idea how to dress. They arrive with only the things they stand in, dirty jeans, scuffed shoes, that sort of thing. So I have one room in my house which is all female wardrobe.'

Frannie balked at that. 'I really think I wouldn't want to wear anybody's clothes but my own.'

'Sure you can bring your own gear. I'll bet you know more or less what I'd like to have you in. But I warn you, it's liable to get very rumpled.' He lit a cigarette. 'And, uh, messy.'

She pursed her lips. 'I see. Yes, well, I'll bring a change of clothes.'

'Do.' He exposed the print. 'Excellent. You have superb legs, Frannie.'

'See?'

'Sure.' He showed it to her.

'Sexy, no?'

'Sexy, very, yes.' He placed the print face up on the butler's tray, together with the other one. 'Now I shall need a few shots of you naked.'

She swallowed. 'I suppose you will, won't you?'

'Just a few, yes.'

'All right,' she said, slowly. She stood and peeled her dress up over her head, trying to feel elegant about it without seeming to put on a show, a little unnerved by the experience of stripping for a man for reasons other than making love, trying to think of him as a doctor but failing. 'Everything?' she said finally, in a small voice. She was down to her cami-knickers.

'Please.'

But once she had stepped out of her knickers and he told her, full of genuine appreciation and admiration, what a magnificent body she had, she relaxed, beginning at once to feel natural in her nakedness, enjoying the feel of the sun and the breeze on her bare skin. He took several shots of her by the ornamental pool. She posed well, and she even found herself surprisingly unembarrassed when the Negro came out to replenish their drinks; besides, he hardly seemed to give her a second glance. But a little later, when Hansom took what was to be the last test shot, what he described as an 'open beaver', her in the deckchair, legs wide, hands between them spreading herself, she knew that the Negro was watching from a window and this knowledge, combined with blatently sexual opening up to the camera and the man behind it, contrived to make her suddenly very horny.

But Hansom said, 'Okay, that'll do, you can get dressed now.' And she found herself disappointed. The experience had finally turned into a new high for her and he was unwittingly cutting it short just as it had started, she dared, 'Do you mind if I don't? I'd like to enjoy the sun a little longer.'

'Sure. But not too long. That sun is deceptive and I like that superb skin just the colour it is.' He had all the prints, there were sixteen of them,, laid out side by side on the tray and he studied each one in turn while Frannie lay back, an arm behind her head stretching taut her breasts, her eyes closed to the sun. After a while he said, 'I'm getting an idea for the scene. And probably the guys to do it. If you'll go along with it, that is.'

Frannie opened one eye. 'Which is?'

'First, I have to say you have one of the most beautiful bodies I've ever photographed. Whoever I picture you making love with has to be young, lean and muscular.'

She opened her other eye. 'Sounds nice.' Her voice dropped half an octave.

'Good. I want some wild sex pictures. Real horny stuff, you know? But I want them to be beautiful as well. Handsome, clean cut young men, expensive clothes, beautiful locations.' His eyes roved around the garden. 'I haven't shot too much in the open air lately. And the sunshine this time of the year gives the very best light. I think perhaps we'll begin with a friendly stroll through the woods down the road to begin with. All of you together, laughing, touching, happy, that sort of thing ...'

Frannie interrupted, eyes wide. '*All* of us?' She hesitated. 'You mean two couples, or more?'

Hansom smiled easily at her, flashing his too-perfect teeth. 'Not exactly. I thought three men and you, as a matter of fact.'

'Oh.' Frannie felt a little weak, but the randyness was still there, increasing if anything as she lay naked next to this rather charming stranger listening to him so casually explaining the plans he was developing for the sexual use of her body.

'Do you go along with the idea so far?'

She wriggled, realized that she was getting damp between her legs. 'I guess I do.'

'Great. Now, the next bit you might have objections to, and it's not imperative. Your skin has a marvellous texture to it and to show it at its best it needs contrast.' He paused. 'I think that two of those young men should be black.'

'Oh.' Frannie even weaker, picturing the wedding anniversary present of the previous year, Lord Ballington and the two coloured men, that incredibly steamy night of sex.

'How do you feel about it?'

She turned limpid, drooping eyes on him, thinking. How do I *feel* about it? You should *know*. I feel totally turned on, that's how I feel. I wish you'd get your trousers down and fuck me right now. She said, trying

62

to keep the quiver out of her voice, 'It's all right. I'll do it.'

'Fine. Fine!' The way he said it, she had just agreed to accept a delightful surprise, not to be photographed in an orgy with three men. 'It could be my best sequence ever. We'll do it this way, I'll have my best writer work on the text. Something like, ah, we'll have you be an English Lady, just as your are, you're on holiday in the States, borrowing an absent friend's house. I'll hire a Rolls for it, the introduction text will be that you picked up three football players at a party at a country club after a match the previous night, you've invited them to the house next day for sex. That's how it should start, all arriving at the house in the Rolls. You'll wear, let me think, have you got something clinging, very chic, scarlet perhaps?'

Frannie was finding his enthusiasm catching. She nodded. 'From Givenchy. In Paris. It's terribly sexy.'

'Good. And the highest heels you've got, to match. Simple, but alluring underwear. White, I think, another fine contrast with those ebony skins.'

'*Ebony*?'

'Sure. The guys I have in mind are *very* black. They shine.' Frannie made a little grunting sound and her buttocks tightened under her. 'They'll play around with you a bit in the woods, you know, general fooling around, probably get to have your knickers down, one of their cocks comes out, that sort of thing. The *real* action we'll set right here in the garden. Near the pond. No. Better still, with the rose-garden in the background, a mass of colour. I'll work it out properly over the next couple of days.'

Frannie stared across to the rose-garden, trying to imagine what was going to happen to her there. Totally aroused by the images Hansom was putting into her head, by her nakedness with him as he did it, Frannie was now desperately needing sex of one sort or another, and it seemed that David Hansom, with his detached enthusiasm, wasn't about to provide it. She got up, pulled her dress over her head. 'It, um, it all sounds very exciting.' she said. 'By the way, where's the loo?'

'The *what*?'

'The bathroom?'

'Oh, yeah. There's one through the lounge and in the hall, on the left.' She wondered if he realized from her attitude that it wasn't a pee she was in need of.

Frannie found the bathroom where her hand gratefully made its way under the dress and between her legs. Sitting splay-legged on the closed toilet seat she worked two fingers inside herself and began to masturbate urgently as the ball of her thumb caressed her clitoris. She came to a rapid, explosive climax, her back propped against the wall of the owner of *Prick* magazine's bathroom, her eyes closed, as she thought about the things which were to be done to her and photographed for publication in that pornographic monthly.

Frannie did not much care for Miami. Her hotel seethed with the kind of Americans whom she found particularly crass, and the brashness of the place offended her Englishness. She was propositioned several times during the next few days, but by no one who remotely interested her so, with the exception of one impassioned session with Matilda, she stayed celibate.

In the late afternoon of the third day since the test shots she heard from David Hansom: the shooting was provisionally arranged for the following day – could she be there at ten? She was somewhat taken aback when Hansom remarked, in that confidently casual way of his that the young men were 'good, reliable studs', and that they didn't usually have any trouble getting it up so if all went well they should be finished in a day; but she agreed to be there on time which would mean leaving at eight, not an hour which figured in her normal schedule except for sleeping, or at least being in bed. That evening she selected the outfit which she knew would please Hansom, together with a change of clothes as an alternative, three different sets of underwear, each fairly plain but very sexy, two pairs of spiky heeled shoes and some stockings all of which she packed carefully in an overnight bag. She had decided to travel in jeans and a blouse and to drive herself to Sandcut; Frannie did not feel the need for Gregory in this case, seeing nothing to fear from Hansom. There was no need for her bodyguard to hang around there all day long; besides, somehow she did not like the idea of him getting to know what was going on, finding Gregory's little touches of disapproval slightly admonishing, absurd though she knew that was.

She arrived at Hansom's precisely at ten, noticing for the first time that the Stars and Stripes hung from a flagpole at the entrance to his drive, flapping in a breeze which was slightly stronger than it had been on her previous visit. She parked next to a gleaming, silver-grey Rolls and, as she jerked the ring on the bottom of a chain which ran up to a large brass bell outside the front door, her nerves jangled in time with the bell.

Hansom himself opened the door, dressed in neatly cut cream slacks and a blue paisley shirt with puffy sleeves and a big floppy collar and his pleasured smile at welcoming her went a way towards helping her relax. 'Right on time,' he said. 'Excellent. Females are so often late.' He planted a light kiss on her forehead. 'Come on through, the boys are already here.'

Across those highly polished teak floors once again and out through French windows, catching her first sight of three men sitting down by the lake, experiencing a touch of the unreal as if she were standing back and watching herself walk into this situation. The men getting up at their approach, tall, broad-shouldered, lean, pleasant faces, open smiles, two of them very black indeed. Introductions, hand shaking, Frannie confused with herself, the names not registering, her eyes shifting rapidly from man to man to man. They were *very* young, she realized, no more than twenty, any one of them. The white boy looked about seventeen.

Letting herself be led back into the house again, her feet finally finding the floor as Hansom said, 'Let's take a look at your gear. Get you ready.'

In an upstairs room lined on every wall, except for the one with leaded windows overlooking the gardens and Lake Okeechobee, Frannie unpacked her bag onto a bed and Hansom inspected the contents with an approving eye. He held the scarlet Givenchy dress against her, muttering, 'Perfect. Just perfect,' then surprised her by adding, 'But your nails are a little pale. They should be darker. Here.' Opening a closet door he searched in a drawer and produced three bottles of nail varnish each one of which he compared with the material of the dress. Then he handed her a bottle. 'This one. It's absolutely right. You don't mind?'

Frannie shook her head. 'Of course not.' She looked at the bottle. 'Are you always so meticulous?'

'The secret of my success, my dear. That's why my magazine's the biggest seller of its kind in America.' Which was true, but in fact had little to do with the colour of his girls' nail varnish, which Hansom knew; he always had a new model paint her nails, harbouring a theory that the act of nail-painting helped to relax her.

'I'll do them once I'm dressed,' said Frannie.

'Fine.' Hansom picked up a fine satin bra, dropped it

again. 'This set of underwear and the darker of the shoes.' He went to another drawer, producing a cellophane packet. 'I'd like you to wear these stockings, you'll find that they're your size and of course they're new. Oh, and one last touch.' He produced something from his shirt pocket. 'Please stick this on your thigh. About there.' He touched her jeans, high up on the inside of her leg, and handed her a small blue transfer, about the size of a large postage stamp. It was of a tiger's head, the tiger showing its teeth.

'How does it work?' Asked Frannie.

'You let it soak for a few moments. Like this.' A saucer of water was standing on a bedside table, and he placed the transfer carefully on its surface. 'On second thoughts *I'd* better do it. Drop your jeans.'

Frannie stared silently at him. The intimacies were starting, right here in this room. Well, this is what she was here for. Unbuckling her crocodile-skin belt, Frannie unzipped her fifteen hundred dollar designer jeans, the sound of the zip loud to her ears, slid them down her legs and stepped out of them. Underneath she was wearing pale blue silk panties, not quite transparent. But Hansom was not watching her, he was removing the transfer from the saucer. Going to Frannie he crouched in front of her and gently placed the transfer on her inner thigh. The touch of his fingers in so intimate a spot, just below where the ends of a few pubic hairs curled under the edge of her panties made Frannie's thigh muscles tighten and she pushed herself fractionally toward him.

Making no comment on her reaction he said, as he carefully slid off the backing paper, 'A lot of girls are having the real thing done today, in all sorts of intimate places. They think it's very sexy. So do I. But I don't think it should be permanent, a tattoo. There.' He stood. 'Perfect. And it comes off with a bit of alcohol. See you in the garden shortly.' He turned and left.

'Yes, I suppose you will,' Frannie muttered to the closing door. She glanced down at her thigh. There *did* seem to be something especially sexy about the dark blue, angry tiger's head. She removed her panties, clipped on a suspender belt and unwrapped the stockings; they were a very light shade of rose, close to colourless, a fine seam ran down their backs and they were adorned in the area of the side of the shin with what appeared to be hand-painted flowers. Frannie liked them immediately; whatever else this man Hansom had, he had a certain flair.

Ten minutes later she was walking awkwardly down the crazy paving which traversed the lawn, shaking her hands briskly at waist level to encourage the freshly varnished nails to dry, uncomfortably aware that the eyes of all the men at the water's edge were watching her every step. There was a fifth man now, bald and quite fat who at first glance she did not much like the look of.

As she reached the group Hansom said, 'Sensational. Truly sensational.' There was a general murmur of assent. Then he said, 'This is Gerry, my photographer and assistant. Though today I'll be taking the photos and Gerry'll be helping me.'

Gerry said, 'Hi,' and grinned at her, and his face seemed all right then. He added, 'What an extremely gracious young lady, if you don't mind me saying so.' And Frannie realized that he was English and found that she did not mind him at all.

Hansom said, 'Something missing. At least for the opening shots.'

'A hat, perhaps?' Gerry suggested.

'Ah, yes. A hat.' He hurried across the lawn and into the house.

One of the coloured boys said, 'How do you feel

about today, honey?'

Frannie smiled briefly at him. 'I can't really say. A little weird I suppose.'

'You ever done it before?'

'Done it? Oh, I see what you mean. Er, posed, no.'

'Don't worry. You're gonna enjoy it. We're gonna be *real* good to you. You'll see.'

'Oh.' Quietly. A crooked smile.

Hansom reappeared, a hat in either hand. One was floppy black felt, the other a straw, summery affair with a colourful band around it. He tried them both on her, settled for the straw number. Then he said, 'Okay, ready to roll. Let's do it.'

They all trooped through the house to the Rolls, the inevitability of the situation stirring Frannie's nervous system; this was the point-of-no-return. Hansom had Frannie get behind the wheel with the boys as passengers and he took several shots of them driving towards the house and pulling into the drive. Then he froze Frannie in three inelegant attitudes leaving the car, no relation to the way she normally slid from car seats, knees carefully together. He had her pose with legs apart, dress rucked high up her thighs, underwear showing and it was her first intimation of the sort of photographic technique to come, the having to move into the exact position Hansom wanted and hold it right there.

Those shots finished, Hansom got behind the wheel and they all squeezed in to drive two miles down the road where there was a pine forest. He parked in a secluded lane and they made their way through the trees, springy bed of dry pine needles crackling underfoot, to a sunlit glade with a long-dead fallen tree. Here Hansom took a number of distance shot, from a hundred yards or so away, the four of them running, laughing, Frannie barefoot, holding hands with two of them, the third close behind, holding her shoes.

They started into the sex. Frannie, who still had to loosen up, to let go and enjoy whatever was to happen to her, found her perverse nature conspiring to make her try and be cold and indifferent.

The initial shot, her backed against a tree, one black youth with a hand under her skirt, the white boy fondling her breast, she physically ignored, her mind forcing itself elsewhere. The setting was shot several times from different angles; they were posed in two slightly variant attitudes, and had to hold them. Once Gerry carefully adjusted Frannie's hat.

But as the posing became progressively more sexually explicit, Frannie found it increasingly difficult not to involve her mind with what was happening to her body. Yet the more she let herself enjoy what was happening to her, the more frustrated she became at the need to pose, to be quite still while various shots were taken. She had no idea it would be like this; she had had the notion that they would all be screwing, more or less freely, while Hansom took picture after picture.

The stillness was not so bad in the scene before last where they had her bent over the old fallen tree, knickers at the back of her knees, two of the boys in the act of pulling them down, the third watching. The sun was warm on her bare arse and she was beginning to feel thoroughly dirty, her exhibitionist streak perversely roused, the fact of five pairs of male eyes and a camera on her naked behind sweetly exciting. The worst frustrations came in the final scene. Hansom had her sitting in the fork of a tree, knickers hanging from one ankle, legs splayed, one coloured boy on his knees, his face buried in her crotch, the other one planting a kiss on her cheek while she held his not quite erect but very large member in her hand as the white boy played with an exposed breast from behind her. Her juices were beginning to flow, she wanted to

70

*move*, to grind her crotch into the kneeling boy's mouth, to take that black cock and wank it and suck it real good, make it good and hard, but was made to keep still for eternal moments, an agony of self-control as Hansom and his camera moved around the group, taking shot after shot after endless shot. Finally he said, flashing his teeth, 'Great. Okay, kids you can relax now.' *Relax*! 'That winds up the woods scene. A spot of lunch, I think.' He might as well have been photographing the mating habits of squirrels.

On the drive back, Frannie subdued, squeezed in behind with the three boys, each one of whom now knew every intimate part of her body. Confused and uncomfortable. It had, of course been a turn on. But it had also been clinical, and in some ways a turn-*off* and frustrating as hell. Even now, potent masculinity pressed close around her, cocks she had handled, she would be happy to get into some heavy sex, she would have *loved* to get to work on those boys, but it wasn't part of the deal and there was, in any case, the affable Hansom chatting away happily about how successful he thought the morning's work had been, while Gerry was remembering aloud some of the technical aspects and she was obliged to sit there silently nursing her thoughts and emotions.

Lunch was a fairly quiet affair, served on the verandah of the house, somehow an awkward intrusion in the day's happenings, the boys' remarks, when they made any at all, seeming to be forced. Only Hansom and Gerry were completely at ease, nobody mentioned sex.

They had coffee, then sat by the lake for half an hour. Then Hansom said, 'Okay you guys, time for the main action. The light couldn't be better. Gerry and I will set it up first. Call you when we're ready.'

Frannie watched in silence as Gerry carried the mattress from a lounger to the rose garden and

Hansom fetched some silver-papered reflector boards and some clamps from the house. The two fussed around for a while, setting up the boards, checking the scene through camera viewfinders and then Hansom appeared satisfied, calling Frannie and the others over.

Hansom smiled at Frannie. He said, bluntly, 'Now Frannie, you understand that you're about to get thoroughly laid by these guys? It's going to be quite a scene?'

She nodded, saying nothing. But the boldness of his words brought a familiar lump of anticipation to her throat.

'Let's do it. Guys, I want you stripped from the waist down, no socks, shirts knotted. And I want to see those pricks upstanding. Frannie, please darling, pants off and tuck your dress into your belt. Get rid of the hat, put your shoes on. And here,' he handed her a brush. 'Give your hair a good brushing. I'll have to clip it somehow, there's a little too much wind. But pants off first. Give the boys a reason to get it up.'

Frannie stepped out of her knickers and rucked her skirt up into her belt, feeling, though her knickers had already been down several times that day, very exposed. She began brushing her hair, the three boys standing near to her, watching her, playing with themselves. One of the black boys already had a hard-on, it was good and big and he stroked it with almost loving attention. The white boy was almost there, too, he was working steadily at it; only the second black boy was jerking at a still flaccid penis. Frannie finding herself getting very turned on again, part of a strange, coldly erotic scene, the unrealness of which was intensified, as was her horniness, when Hansom pulled her dress up even higher and fixed her hair as the boys continued to play with their cocks. The other black boy was almost erect now.

'Right,' said Hansom. 'Let's get a good group scene

going. Benji, on your back on the mattress, please. Frannie, you straddle him. Get that thing inside you.' He watched as she knelt over him. 'Are you wet enough?'

Frannie was almost too eager. She heard herself saying, 'Of *course* I'm fucking wet enough!' Impaling herself on the thick, black tool, sliding right down on it, hearing Hansom as he said, 'Remember, nobody comes inside the lady. Anybody wasting a cum shot like that loses pay.'

Moving, the boy quite still, sliding that prick in and out of her, letting go, but immediately stopped, Hansom's hand stilling her, almost desperate with the need to move, to *fuck*. Hansom crouched beside her, mouth close to her ear, very quietly saying, 'Frannie, do you object to anal sex?'

Frannie, the question increasing her arousal, moving again up and down that shaft, stopped once more, moaning. 'Anything, do anything', a finger slipping into her other hole, a greasy feeling, making her squirm. Vaseline. The white boy, legs apart, beginning to intrude his cock into her arse, a little pain, gone. Freeze right there, says Hansom. Perfect. Circling, camera clicking, Frannie not daring to move, gasping as she feels herself impaled fully by the white boy, two cocks all the way in her now, trying to move, unable, the other black cock shoved at her face, then filling her mouth. Freeze! Like that! And the keeping still becomes a diabolical, exquisite torture, endless, as the boys changed position, taking turns in each others places, the process, the agony, protracted because a cock fresh from her arse must be washed before moving on.

Finally. Finally. The coming. No more 'freeze'. Okay in your mouth Frannie? Over your face? Sure. Please. *Please*. Give me that cum. One black cock spurting over her cheeks, her neck, finally warm, spicy cum in her mouth, couched in her tongue. Now, *smile*, Frannie, *smile*! At the camera! Doing it, as another cock sprays her lips and the third shoots all over her neck and breasts. *Smile!*

It's over. The man has all the pictures he needs. But not for Frannie, it's not. Licking her lips, taking more cum in her mouth, rubbing her hands over sticky breasts, smelling the musky, horny smell. At fever-pitch excitement. She wants a *fucking*. A good hard *fucking*, where she can *move* for Christ's sake. She dares, desperation. 'Please, can't we just carry on?'

'Sure we can, Frannie. Anything you like.' Pause. 'I make it a rule never to get involved with my models.' Again the pause. 'Until *after* a shoot, that is. What you need now is a truly experienced, mature *man*.' Quietly, but with power.

And David Hansom helps her to her feet, takes her by the elbow and leads her, crumpled dress still tucked high up into her belt, across the lawn, into the house and upstairs to his bedroom.

# 5
# Ain't Misbehavin'

Frannie stared languidly up at her image which gazed back at her with equal languor from the crumpled bed reflected on the ceiling. She smiled. The mirror covered the entire ceiling and the evidence of their earlier haste was plain: his paisley shirt a screwed-up ball near her head, his underpants and trousers lying in a heap with his shoes at the foot of the bed, and her dress, suspender belt and stockings trailing to the floor in abandoned disarray.

Alone, she looked around what was a quite extraordinary bedroom. The mirrored ceiling extended down the wall to the floor behind the bed and on another wall was a framed collage at least ten feet long by five feet deep, of pornographic photographs. The bed, a gigantic affair, was a water-bed, an experience Frannie was enjoying for the first time in her life, and its linen was black. A luxurious snowy-white wool carpet stretched, in obvious contrast to the bed, from wall to wall and in one corner of the room, close to the windows, was an almost life-sized sculpture, beautifully executed in pink marble, of a naked women on her knees performing fellatio on an equally naked man. Set into the wall facing the foot of the bed, some twelve feet away from it, was the biggest TV screen she had ever seen, extensive video and sound equipment, and a video and tape library.

A door opened and David Hansom appeared, a

small white towel draped around his middle, a full glass in either hand. For such a big man he was surprisingly trim and there was no excess fat on him anywhere; a thatch of grey hair on his chest matched that on his head. He handed her a glass which she took without moving from the position her naked body had arranged itself in after her third orgasm: knees doubled, lying sideways to the rest of her body, looking just as if she had been posed like that by a photographer intending to depict sexual contentment.

Hansom said, 'Your beer, your ladyship. Strange sort of request in this situation. But I've decided to join you.' He sipped from his glass then sat at the foot of the bed facing her, one leg doubled under him, the other foot on the floor.

Frannie propped herself up on the pillows and then drank deeply from the glass. 'Good. Good and cold,' she said. 'I'm unbelievably thirsty.'

'You bet you are.' He stared at her. 'So, what did you think of today?'

She pondered, pursing her lips, the trace of a wicked smile appearing. 'Amusing. Extraordinary, of course. Weird.' She paused. 'But I guess I have to rate the last part best.' Hansom permitted herself a small smile but said nothing. 'On the other hand, I doubt if it would have been quite the same without what went before, if you see what I mean.'

'Excessive frustration?'

'You might have warned me.'

He grunted. 'Women react differently. I saw what it was like with you while it was happening, but I had no way of knowing beforehand.'

'Come *on*. Surely it's like that with most women. It *has* to be.'

'Most, no. Perhaps half. Maybe a little more.'

'And the rest?'

'Seem to take it in their stride. Well, I can't speak for

76

their minds, but their bodily reaction, most certainly.' He sipped his beer, then grinned fleetingly. 'But you, my dear, were something else. Like a thoroughbred racehorse straining to be through the starting gate.'

She laughed at the analogy. 'Damned frustrating. *Damned* frustrating!'

'Would you do it again?'

'Possibly. Certainly not for a while.' She frowned. 'But tell me something, is it so necessary for your models to keep still?'

'Absolutely. It's the only way I can be sure of capturing the very best pictures. Some of my cheaper rivals shoot stills of action sex, but it's poor stuff. And I *do* sell as many magazines as everyone else in the field together.'

'Good for you. But what's the legal situation? I mean, in England it's all under the counter stuff, even in sex shops. Totally ridiculous, of course. I mean, everyone one knows enjoys a spot of porn.'

'Yeah. In the States we have an extremely confused situation. It's only strictly legal in New York and California. Here, in Florida, like in many other states it's tolerated, but if somebody really wants to get nasty you can still walk into trouble. And there are other places, those old Methodist enclaves, where I swear they'd hang you for it if they got their hands on you. My situation is a bit – well, not a bit, a lot – like Larry Flint's.'

'Who's he?'

'*Hustler* magazine. Law suits all over the country, all the time. Same with me. But it's worth it. I'm fighting for more than the bread.'

'Oh?'

'Believe it or not, there's a principle here. Why shouldn't we be allowed to publish pictures of human sexual activity? A hell of a lot of people want to see them. And those that don't don't have to look. A lot of people don't want to see pictures of football or tennis, so they don't buy football or tennis magazines. Sex is something almost everybody frequently indulges in in one form or another, and quite often looking at pictures of other men and women screwing adds spice. I believe that to be perfectly healthy.'

'Then what about anal sex, sucking, group scenes like today's?'

'The first and the second are practised by the majority of sexually healthy human beings. The third, perhaps not, but looking at pictures of it caters for a widely held, but largely unfulfilled fantasy.' He paused. 'Tell me something. How do you feel when you open what is a well-known, mass circulation magazine and are suddenly confronted with the colour picture of someone blown apart by a bomb, or an execution, or mutilated corpses after an air disaster?'

Frannie grimaced. 'Revolted. I turn the page.'

'You turn the page. But, too late – you've already been exposed to the picture, like it or not. Unnatural human activity, violence, ugliness. If any pictures should be banned, it's those. Instead of which, they're thrust at you.

'My magazine is sold in a clear plastic wrapper; kids can't browse through it on newsstands. There is no doubt as to its content. You take it or you leave it.'

'I entirely agree with your sentiments. That is, provided it's not kiddy porn; or animals, stuff like that.'

'Right. Again, unnatural practises.'

'What about homosexuality?'

'Male homo is a specialised field. A big one, which I'm not into. But lesbianism is something else. Most readers of my magazine like to see two women together, even the women. I've never come to any real conclusion why men together are almost exclusively enjoyed in magazines by male homosexuals. Why men

78

like to see women together and women don't like to see men.'

Frannie shrugged. 'Maybe because it emasculates them. Women making love to each other look generally feminine.'

'You may have something there.'

'But, personally, I like to see the occasional picture of queers at it. It has its own special turn-on.'

'Is there anything which *doesn't* turn you on?'

'Not a lot. I think I already told you.'

'Right.' He shifted position, unintentionally opening up the towel and giving Frannie a full view of his male equipment. Despite the indulgences of the day her eyes were attracted to it; he made no attempt to cover up. He said, 'I've a great idea for you. How would you like to be photographed having sex, but moving?'

'I don't know. Well, I guess I would.'

'Sure you would. Will you please pass me the telephone?' It was on the bedside table. She stretched for it and handed it to him. As she leant forward, her breasts dangled pertly. He punched numbers and said, 'I've got a pal in California who makes sex videos. Good ones. Can you make California?'

She tossed her head. 'I'm free to go wherever I like.'

'I'll see what his schedule is.'

Hansom got through and spoke for two or three minutes, Frannie getting more than half the sense from hearing one end of the conversation. Then he said 'Hold on, she's right here with me,' and put one hand over the mouthpiece. 'Frannie, can you get there in the next couple of days?' She nodded. 'And then back again in a few weeks time for ten days or so?'

She looked puzzled. 'Why again?'

'He's auditioning now to shoot in seven weeks.'

'Oh, I see. Well, fine.'

Hansom spoke briefly to California then hung up. 'It's fixed. You'll get a part for sure.'

'Sounds like fun.'

'For you, the best.' He drained his glass. 'How come you're so mobile?'

'Little plaything called a Lear jet. Belongs to my husband.' And she told him about her round the world sex trip.

When she finished he said, 'Truly amazing. I never heard anything like that before. I should come with you, recording it all for *Prick*.'

She looked at him archly. 'And have me keep still all the time? No way!'

He laughed. 'You have a point there.'

'By the way, how do you do it? I mean, don't you get turned on all the time taking those pictures?'

'No. Not at all. It's strictly a job at the time. I have a trick of blanking my mind. Getting it absolutely right is my one and only consideration.'

'Amazing. But you sure were turned on today.'

'Afterwards, yes. When the shooting was over with. But that only happens if I fancy one of the women involved. In your case it was pretty obvious it had to happen.' She glanced at his genitals again; her look was like a physical touch and he felt a stirring.

Seemingly reluctantly she slowly shifted her gaze back to his face. 'Any chance of getting some prints of today before I leave?'

'They're being processed right now. But if you wait two or three months I'll send you the magazine.'

'That long?'

'I always work three copies ahead.'

'Oh. Well, thank you. But I'd like to send some prints to my husband shortly, if you can manage it. Prove to him what a good time I'm having.'

'Jesus, Frannie, you're one amazing lady. Sure, I'll let you have some prints.'

'Thank you.' She paused. 'Do you really find me amazing?' Her gaze returned to between his legs. 'It

80

seems you do. Something seems to be happening down there. Again.'

'With you around, how can I help it?'

'Mmmm. Quite.' Frannie moved forward onto her knees then eased herself down flat on her belly, her hands on his thighs moving the towel completely aside as she said huskily, looking briefly into his eyes then back at his almost hard cock. 'That needs a thorough sucking.'

Looking down at her as she took his cock full in her mouth, at her blonde hair cascading shiningly over her shoulders, her slender back and beautifully proportioned derriére, her long, slim legs, feeling her warm mouth drawing hungrily at him, her tongue busy, he murmured, 'What else could I call my magazine but *Prick*? – What else is there?'

# 6
# California, Here I *Come*

Frannie naked except for a pair of black, high-heeled, peep-toe shoes, supine on the emerald green coverlet of a double bed. Over her head, a microphone dangling from a boom. At the foot of the bed a youngish man, beard, long hair, wearing a track suit, was down on one knee, his shoulder supporting a video camera which was aimed between Frannie's legs. At one side of the bed, six feet away from it, was an older man, jeans and t-shirt, darkly tanned, also with a video camera, standing, the camera sloping from his shoulder towards the undressed Frannie. The scene was bathed in white light from three powerful arc-lamps. Behind the light, a dark shadow, Bernard Goldberg, ageing producer and director of sex films. With Goldberg was his pillar-of-society stockbroker buddy Alan Hirsh, on set solely for prurient reasons.

Goldberg, voice raised, says, 'Okay. We're ready to roll, Frannie. Let's see it just like I told you.'

Frannie's two hands caressing her breasts, lovingly watching herself do it, pushing them together with the heels of her hands so they bulge forward, rolling them slowly up and down, one against the other. Careful not to look at the cameras, pinching her nipples, then running the hands down across her flat belly, a little gasp as the fingers encounter pubic hair. Eyes closing, tongue wetting lips, both hands at her crotch. Making little mewling, moaning sounds. Exactly the attitude required by the director but not, as he had suggested, pretending she is alone with a dirty book, rather totally aware of the fact of all those men watching her, doing it for their benefit, therefore for her own, turning herself deliciously on, no act this, a wet Frannie bringing herself to what is to be a quick, consuming orgasm. Fingers moving faster, faster, legs beginning to shudder, to open and close, moans getting louder, a twisting of her body, an involuntary heaving of her buttocks, a gasp, a groan. Stillness. Vaguely aware of a stage-whisper, Alan Hirsh, the only man present with a hard-on. 'Jeesus. You've found yourself a natural here, Bernie. What a shiksa!'

Goldberg saying, 'Okay, cut. Great, Frannie. Great stuff. But when I shoot a scene like that in the film we'll need it to last a bit longer. But as good an act as any I've seen.'

Frannie, opening limpid, blue eyes, peering into the shadows beyond the lamps. Wicked, as so often. 'What act? That was for real.' Invoking another 'Jeeesus!' from the stockbroker.

'Tony. On set, please.' From Goldberg. And a young, naked man, penis flaccid, appears. He smiles at her. 'Hi.'

She smiles back. 'Hello.'

'Let's hear how you deliver, Frannie.' Goldberg materialises. He is thin. He has on a flowered silk shirt, open to the waist, heavy gold chains adorn his hairy, skinny chest, a solid gold Rolex nestles in a clump of hairs at his wrist. He hands them a sheet of paper each, identical, a page of script. 'Read it through a couple of times, get the feel of it, you know, let me know when you're ready.'

They both study the lines; at one point Frannie feels the giggles coming on, suppresses them. After a while Tony says, 'Okay?' and Frannie nods.

'From the top, then,' says Goldberg. 'Quiet on set. Roll the tape.'

*Dick*
What are we doing sitting here
with our clothes on, Myra?
*Myra*
You have a better idea,Dick?
*Dick*
Sure. Why don't we fuck?
*Myra*
Okay. But I'd like to play around
a little first. You know.
*Dick*
Why don't you tell me exactly
what you want us to do?
Spell it out.
*Myra*
You a listening freak? You
like to have girls talk dirty?
*Dick*
Yeah.
*Myra*
Okay. Here's what we're going
to do. First you lift up my
dress and pull my panties down.
I open my legs and you get your
head down there, stick your
tongue in my cunt. When I'm
real wet I'll unzip your pants,
take out your cock, toss you
off a little, take it in
my mouth …

In weirdland again. Frannie's delivery good, even
though she considers the lines a little ridiculous.
Saying them the way she thinks she *would* say them,
but at the same time very conscious of a totally strange
situation, an unreality. This can't be me, surrounded
by cameras and men and lights, naked, with a naked

man, both of us calmly reading aloud from a banal dirty script which has something to do with a scene which will happen, or already has happened some other time. She is reminded of Kafka.

Yet it's for real. They reach the bottom of the page of script and Goldberg says, 'Fine. Cut the sound. Let's get some action rolling.' A hand from the shadows, pointing, the Rolex glinting. 'You'll need to do something about that, Tony.'

Tony still limp. 'Oh, yeah.' Just like the three boys of two days previously, he now stands looking at her, stroking his penis.

'Why don't you give him a little help, Frannie?' From the shadows.

Frannie, ever ready to oblige; he's a good-looking young man and his sexual equipment attracts her mouth like lodestone. He quickly begins to go rigid in it, as with one hand she cups his balls, the other steals around his arse.

'Let's roll.' The cameras moving in on the action, circling, Tony's eight inches filling Frannie's mouth, switching her right on.

'That's enough. All fours on the bed, Frannie, Tony, kneel behind her, legs apart so that we can see what's going on, just enough, you know the form. And I want one camera right in there, in close-up. Okay, slide it in her, all the way. Now, *pump*. Good and steady. In-out, in-out, in-out, in-out.' Goldberg thumping a balled fist into the palm of his hand as he establishes this rhythm. 'Frannie, arch your back as much as you can, *thrust* back at him, close your eyes and head back, move it around. *Perfect*. Mutter to yourself, you're getting carried away, you're saying dirty words.'

Frannie is thoroughly immersed in this now; of course she's getting carried away. The difference between being on camera for stills and for a movie was incredible, considering they were both the same subject, both had those added spices to normal sex of an audience, cameras, instructions. But now she could really let herself go, now she could fuck on camera – the big element missing from the stills.

'Okay. Change of position. On your back, Frannie. Missionary. Take the weight on your hands, Tony, body well clear of her. Steady rhythm again. Reach down Frannie, between his legs, give his balls a squeeze. Good. Now both hands on his arse, let's see those immaculate nails *digging* into the flesh. Great stuff. Now, Tony, *thrust*. All the way in, and *hold* it. Still, for one, two and three seconds. Now, quickly out and *bang* it in again. Hold it there, hold it there. One, two, three. *Bang*! Now, again. Frannie, shout as he does it, roll your head around, eyes wide, mouth open. You're an *animal*!'

Goldberg so carried away by his direction that he seems not to notice that Frannie *is* shouting, her head is rolling and her eyes and mouth are wide as she comes to a beautiful climax and keeps right on moving. This is *too* much.

It's too much for Alan Hirsh as well. His cock has been straining in his trousers for quite long enough and he disappears in search of the toilet.

They go through more positions. Goldberg has them perform sixty-nine, side-by-inverted-side, then Frannie has to get down on the carpet and bend over the bed, Tony spearing her again from behind.

Goldberg appearing in the light. 'Anal okay, Frannie?'

Frannie, eager. 'Mmmm.'

Then a disappointment, immediately forgotten as Tony thrusts powerfully into her, when Goldberg continues, 'Great. But leave it out, Tony, we don't need it for the test shots.'

Finally, 'Let's wrap it up. Frannie. I want to see how you take a cum-shot. Lean back against the wall, legs straight, apart. Good. Now, Tony, kneel over her thighs. Now, take that prick and suck him right off, Frannie. *Do* it!'

Frannie needing no encouragement. Using one hand and her mouth, working on him, feeling him tensing, nearing orgasm as her other hand, uninstructed, finds its way down between her legs, two fingers sliding inside her. Final muscular spasms from Tony. Grunts. Pelvic muscles, thighs, knotting like iron. A heaving against her.

Goldberg, tripping over his words in his anxiety to get them said in time. '*Now*, get it out of your mouth, let's *see* that cum. Keep a hold on his cock. *Direct* the cum. Don't look at the camera.' And, as Tony starts to spurt. '*Get* it, Frannie, in your mouth, over your lips, then your tits. And close your eyes. This is *ecstacy*!'

Ecstacy indeed. Holding tight onto that cock, squeezing it, feeling it pulsate as she jerked her hand on it, directing the flood of warm cum where Goldberg wanted it to go, just the way she might have done it in any case had the two of them been alone.

'Beautiful. Cut. That's it.' The lights go out, but Frannie keeps hold of Tony's still-erect member. He's slumped into the wall, his cheek against it. Her mouth, the lipstick smeared with sperm, takes in the end of his cock once more, sucking the last drops from it as she furiously masturbates herself to yet another explosive climax, oblivious to all else as the crew begin to clear away their equipment and Alan Hirsh returns from the toilet, eyes bulging once more as he catches this final, unfilmed act.

Moments of soul-searching. Frannie, in a penthouse suite of the Beverly Hills Hotel stood by the window looking out over the sprawling city. There was a heavy blanket of cloud, a few drops of rain in the air; it made her think of England.

Goldberg, secretly delighted with her on-screen performance, but fairly non-committal about it to her face – the manner of producers the world over out to pay the smallest possible fee – had offered her a part in his movie. It was a biggish one which would require her to make love with, in various combinations, several men, at least six, and she had accepted. But now, perhaps it was the weather, heavy clouds always seemed to press a little on her, she wondered about the wisdom of that decision. It was occurring to her just how far she had already pushed her sexual bounds on this trip, just over a week old; she had loosed emotions which even she, a highly experienced, sexually liberated woman, had not been aware could exist. Was there not perhaps some hidden danger in all this indulgence? Could it turn into a drug, something she would have to depend increasingly on and need in bigger doses as time went by? She was on a fantastic sexual high and now she considered where, if anywhere, it was leading her. Admittedly, only a slight touch of doubt, but the seeds were there on this dismal afternoon, and they irritated her.

She crossed the room to where a slim, crocodile-skin handbag lay on a stone coffee table, her irritation unrelieved by the Roman Era theme of the suite, an example of typical American extravagance. In the bag she had some of the prints from the David Hansom shooting which she intended to post off that afternoon to Lord Ballington. Hansom had let her have copies of ten of what he considered the best photos and she went slowly through them, the actuation fresh in her mind.

There was one picture which she stared at for a long time. It was sharp and clear, the colour excellent. She was on hands and knees on the mattress in front of the rose garden. It was a three-quarter rear shot, a tableau with the two black young men, one supine beneath her, his penis inside her, the other crouched behind her, knees on either side of her as he penetrated her rear end. She was glancing back at the camera, a happy smile on her face, a smile that *worked* yet contradicted her real emotions at that moment – the desperate need to have everybody concerned to be allowed to *move*.

Matilda appeared. For a moment Frannie made to hide the photos, then she thought better of it.

'What are your plans for this evening, Frannie?' Matilda asked.

'I hadn't thought about it. But since you ask, why don't we go somewhere nice to eat together? It seems to me we haven't done that in ages.'

Matilda looked pleased and surprised. 'That'll be smashing. Not man-chasing, then?'

'I think I'll give it a miss. I've had a tiring three days.'

'Oh? How was the screen test?'

'Ah, yes. The screen test. I don't believe I mentioned what *type* of test it was, did I? Or what those so-called fashion photos were all about, did I?'

'No. So, tell me then.'

'Yes. Actually, I need your opinion. I could, of course, phone Victor, but I think he'll be merely amused. I know he will.' She handed Matilda the prints. 'What do you think of these?'

On top was a shot of Frannie bending over the fallen tree in the glade, bare-arsed, the boys inspecting her. Her face was not in camera.

'*Very* amusing. Nice bum.' Matilda commented. Then she looked at the next one. A close-up of Frannie's face with a cock in her mouth. A black cock. She gasped. 'My God, it's you!'

'Rather.'

'But. Good grief!' She inspected each picture in the little stack, lingering long moments on them, noises of surprise, of amazement. But no intimation of shocked horror. Then she put them down, shaking her head slowly, four eyes inscrutable.

'Well?' From Frannie.

'Bloody horny stuff. About the best I've seen.' She paused. 'And *you*!'

'And me, yes. How about that?'

Matilda pouting, the ghost of a smile. 'You get *all* the fun. Wish it had been me!'

Frannie looked at her in disbelief. 'Is that *all* you have to say?'

'What do you expect? I've been around you a long time, mistress mine. Surprise at anything you get up to lasts about half a minute.'

'I might have known it. You and your penchant for porn.'

'Penchant's an understatement, darling. I adore the stuff!'

'Yes, well. What I want to know, how about me appearing in it? How does that grab you?'

'Unfortunate choice of expression, isn't it?' She picked up one picture again, glanced briefly at it: Frannie with all three. 'Right between the legs, I'd say.'

Frannie giggled, the laughter a welcome relief from self-doubt. 'No, come on, seriously, how do you feel about me doing it? Don't you think I maybe going somewhat over the top?'

Matilda considered. 'Depends. You seem to have done it now anyway. As long as it proved a good way of getting your rocks off, to use a vulgar Americanism. That's what you set out to do, wasn't it? This whole trip?'

'Yes, but ...'

'What but? Your butt.' Pause. 'Did you enjoy it? It certainly looks that way.'

'In a very peculiar sort of way. Yes.'

'Well, then. You should have boundaries, I think even Victor would agree with that. But they should be erected only when you find yourself getting into something you don't want to do. And then very firmly.'

'Yes. Well, that, of course, is Gregory's main function. To get me out of anything which starts going bad.'

'Yet you drove yourself to wherever it was.'

'Funny, I had complete confidence in the man who took those pictures. Funny again, somehow I didn't want Gregory to know about it.'

'I know what you mean. He's a bit of an old woman under that tough exterior.'

'Mmmm.' She paused. 'My screen test was for a porno video.'

'And you got the part?'

'What do you think?'

'And now you're having second thoughts about it?'

'In a way, yes. I don't know it's, it's ...' she shrugged and pulled a rueful little smile. 'Just that I think that maybe I'm being just a touch excessive.'

'Then don't do it. Simple as that.'

'Well, we'll see. I'll think about it closer to the time. It's not for almost a couple of months.' She was feeling better, brighter. Her small confidences with Matilda and her reactions had cheered her. 'Let's go to Europe. Tomorrow.'

Matilda groaned. Real pain. 'We've just got off that damnable plane. We've spent more time up in the blasted air than on the ground.'

'Sorry. But you'll be all right. I've just had a smashing idea. The young man I had the screen test with was quite gorgeous. We had a drink afterwards and he mentioned that he's off to Amsterdam to work in some sort of a sex club there. Some sort of a live show, can you *imagine*? I think I'll surprise him. Give him a lift.' Fishing in her bag, she produced a visiting card. 'Would you mind getting this number for me? There's a darling.'

Bernard Goldberg gave Frannie a number for Tony. She found him in and almost stunned by her offer to fly him to Holland in her private jet, which opportunity he grabbed at.

By the time she hung up, Frannie was feeling quite her usual self again. She smiled teasingly at Matilda. 'You know,' she said. 'It's quite some journey from here to Europe. As I said, Tony's a super-looking young man. Hung like a stud, too. You'll adore him. Take your mind off the flying. We'll probably be able to have a bit of fun with him, you and I. Maybe make one of the home movies while we're at it.'

'Uh uh. And what about friend Gregory?'

'That's a point.' Frannie thought about it. 'He can sit up front with the pilot. No, better, I'll send him ahead, scheduled flight.'

'Frannie, you're incorrigible.'

'No, I'm not. I'm Frannie, Lady Ballington. Remember?' She perched herself on a cushion-strewn sofa, patting the place beside her. 'Let's have a closer look at these.' She picked up the photographs and laid her spare hand on Matilda's thigh, high up, as she sat next to her, squeezing. 'Together.'

# 7
# Birds Do It…

But plans for an airborne sexual frolic with the porn star Tony were dashed for the first leg of their journey to Amsterdam. The 'gorgeous' potent example of young American manhood who met them in the VIP lounge of Burbank Airport was almost unrecognizable as the stud of the previous day's screen test. He was unshaven and haggard, eyes bloodshot, the lids propped open by two very short, invisible sticks. He muttered apologies; he'd been to an all night party, had lost track of the time and barely made it home to get his gear together.

Whatever sort of party he had been to it must have been wild; they could smell it, it was still on him. He reeked of stale cigarette smoke, of sweat and of something else sweet and hard to define which probably had something to do with a mingling of sex and drugs. When she caught that first whiff, right there in the departure lounge, Frannie's pert nose wrinkled in distaste; at that moment she infinitely regretted having invited him along, even had half a mind to cancel the invitation. But his yawned apologies were sufficiently abject and she took him aboard, seating him as far away from Matilda and herself as possible. He promptly fell asleep. As soon as they were allowed to release their seat belts Frannie produced an air freshener from the toilet and sprayed him with it, an action so funny that even Matilda, in

93

her customary state of take-off shock, managed a laugh.

Almost three and a half hours and sixteen hundred miles on they put down briefly for a fuel stop at Chicago. Tony was asleep throughout the operation, and he remained in that condition for the next seven hundred mile leg to Montreal, often breaking into raucous snoring at which time Matilda would shake him, or pinch his nose. He finally came around as they taxied to a halt at Dorval airport, his eyes at least clear and properly open, his apologies profuse. They were obliged to stay overnight in Montreal and Frannie allowed Tony the time to rinse his face, shave and change his clothes before they left the aircraft; but she noticed as they did that there was still a hint of a smell about him. That party had got right into his *skin*! But she insisted in putting him up in a decent room in her hotel; he was her guest and she would pay.

The Tony who appeared at breakfast the next morning came every bit up to Frannie's description of him to Matilda; he had his fair hair washed and trimmed, his squarish chin was clean and shiny, his wide apart, pale green eyes bright and sparkling with intelligence. And there was no doubt that the young man *was* intelligent the fact of his appearances in erotic performances not precluding that.

Over breakfast they questioned him about himself. It seemed he was at acting school and he was also an aspiring novelist. He had had several short stories published in respectable magazines and was struggling with the first book. He lived fairly frugally, his porn work covering the bills, and the stint coming up in a live-show in Amsterdam during holidays from drama school would put a nice lump sum in his bank.

Frannie liked him then, as did Matilda. He was personable, modest, and he had commendable ambition. As a personality, she found it difficult to

94

associate him with the abandoned, on-camera sexual performance of two days before. Then he had been a mere body, highly proficient, acting under instructions. Now the body had a mind, she could look on him with a far more complex interest.

An hour later, as the jet straightened out on its flight-path across the North Atlantic and as her paralysis subsided, Matilda began to look at Tony with a plain, very simple interest, squinting at him through her bi-focals, trying to picture him naked. But it was still a little early in the day for sex; Frannie had that orchestrated for later. Before lunch they watched a movie, the superb celluloid interpretation of James Dickie's 'Deliverance', and, following the Great Circle air route, put down and topped up with fuel after a thousand miles at Gander in Newfoundland in preparation for the longest hop of the journey, the two thousand mile stretch to Shannon, just short of the jet's maximum cruising distance.

Matilda fixed them a marvellous spread. Canapés and Beluga caviar for openers, eased down with a bottle of 1976 Don Perignon, followed by fresh salmon served with a light, clear white wine from the Rioja region of Spain. Then a fruit plate and lastly a well-matured Brie, the cheese complimented by a fine claret from the same region of North-East France. By meal's end they were experiencing the delicious headiness which follows excellent food accompanied by equally superb wine taken in just a touch more than moderation, a feeling connoisseurs believe to be finer than any drug-induced high.

Sipping Turkish coffee, a nip of Napolean brandy in the cup to liven it, Tony said, 'That was great. It sure beats a TWA packed lunch!'

Frannie stretched luxuriously. 'I hope so.' She regarded him with smiling eyes. 'I believe in making these monotonous journeys as agreeable as possible.'

She paused. 'And a good meal is *one* way of helping the day along.' They were in a small dining alcove, where Lord Ballington had had four reclining seats removed from the original lay-out, Frannie across from Tony, Matilda by her side. Keeping her amused eyes on him, tilting her head slightly to one side, Frannie went on, slowly: 'There are of course, *others*. Even more agreeable. What say you, Matilda?'

Matilda treated Tony to what nobody but her knew was a lecherous look. 'Not half. Let me clear the junk away.'

Frannie lit a cigarette, offering one to Tony who refused. 'I only indulge occasionaly after an exceptional meal,' she said. 'Tell me, how did you actually feel, the other day, on camera?'

'The way I usually do, I guess.'

'How's that?'

'Pretty horny.'

'But, not strange in any way?'

'I'm used to the guys around, the cameras, if that's what you mean. I get *very* turned on. Just one thing though. You know sometimes I want to, well, er, you know, to *come*. Having to hold back can be a hell of a strain.'

'So how do you manage it?'

'I put my head somewhere else. Don't laugh, I get a picture of pigs, or of elephants, fixed in my brain. I concentrate on it.'

Frannie looked at him in astonishment. 'And were you thinking of pigs and elephants whilst we were ... *doing* it?'

'Uh, elephants.'

Matilda returned. She had let down her hair and taken off her glasses. 'What about elephants?' she said, staring at Tony who was not to know that from where she stood, four feet away, he appeared as only an indistinct blur.

Frannie chuckled. 'I'll tell you later. But I must say, Tony, I don't find myself terribly flattered.'

'Don't you? With you I was forced to think about elephants most of the time. Actually it's a compliment, if you see what I mean.'

Frannie blinked at him. 'Quite.'

'How extraordinary,' commented Matilda, quite baffled.

'You're going to have to make up for it, you know.' Frannie leant across the table. 'We never did kiss on set, did we?'

'No. We didn't.' His kiss was surprisingly tender, a long exploration of her lips with his, his tongue into play only towards the end.

'My,' she said, resting a hand on his corduroys under the table, high on his thigh, 'That was rather good.' Her hand slid higher, and found what it sought. 'You promise not to think of elephants? Or even of pigs?'

He grinned. 'Promise.'

Frannie moved herself around the table next to him, saying, 'He has a way of kissing, Matilda. You must see for yourself.' Frannie's hand found its way back between his legs, he was getting hard already. 'You, er, you don't mind if Matilda joins us Tony? She can be very enthusiastic.'

'Sounds good.'

Matilda, behind his seat, bent her mouth to Tony's, whilst Frannie's fingers searched for Tony's zipper. What they found were buttons.

'Buttons?' she commented.

Tony broke off his kiss. 'I got fed up with zippers. I just seemed to bust too many.'

'I just bet you did.' Frannie undid his belt buckle and fumbled with the buttons while Tony and Matilda mingled tongues, Matilda rapt with it – she had not actually been kissed in a very long time. Managing the final button, Frannie opened Tony's flies wide. Underneath he was wearing yellow slips of a satiny material, his cock hard and straining against them, and Frannie bent and gave him the heat of her mouth through the material, her lips sideways over his hard-on, teeth nibbling, gently blowing. Matilda meanwhile, whilst still engrossed in her kissing, had contrived to undo her blouse and get her bra down around her waist and, as she offered her voluptuous, snowy-white breasts to Tony, pulling his head down between them, Frannie dragged his pants and trousers together to his knees.

Lear jets are not constructed with sex in mind. Tony could not stand without banging his head, for one thing, which he did when, a little later, his cock having been thoroughly sucked by both ladies, they moved. He had his trousers off now, but not his shirt, his eight inches rigid in front of him, Frannie's pink, Dior pencil skirt was rucked up to her waist and Matilda's tits, the bra removed from around her waist, swung free. Looking for a greater degree of comfort and flexibilty for sexual acrobatics they went forward to the group of six armchair seats.

The Atlantic Ocean, twenty nine thousand feet below them, was disappearing under a high, dark, cloud cover.

'Strip off, Matilda,' said Frannie, thickly. 'Show Tony the rest.' Lowering two of the seats into the fully reclined position she lay back in one, getting Tony to lay in the other, finding it was going to be awkward, the arms would be in the way. She turned on her side, took hold of Tony's cock, masturbating him slowly as they both watched Matilda taking her clothes off, inelegant about it, the plane bumping very slightly twice, making her lurch each time. Then she stood naked in the aisle, her head almost touching the roof, steadying herself against further bumps with a hand on the back of the seat in front of Tony, a feast of expectant, plump white flesh waiting to be gorged on, her thick black thatch of pubic hair overwhelmingly tempting for Tony who sat, reached his hands behind her fleshy buttocks and drew her towards him, tongue searching among the hairs for the right places, finding its way inside her, making her gasp.

The plane bumped again, markedly bigger than before, a scared look flittered across Matilda's face, but then Frannie was saying eagerly, '*Fuck* her Tony. Bend her over the seat and *fuck* her real good.'

Tony on his feet now, leaning over the bending Matilda, his hair brushing the roof, thrusting into her, those powerful, cunt-filling thrusts, the way Goldberg had had him doing it to Frannie, her flesh quivering all over as he bangs it into her while Frannie, eyes greedily devouring the scene, strips off her knickers and plays with herself.

Again a thump, another, and then a violent lurch and ten feet from Matilda's face the seat belt warning light lit up. Matilda moaned, 'Oh Christ, Oh *Christ*,' not because of the prick inside her but because of the sudden panic in her as the pilot's voice, calm, addressed them over the intercom. 'Nothing to be in the least alarmed about, Lady Ballington, but there's some pretty foul weather below us. There's going to be quite a bit of turbulence. Please buckle your seat belts and put the seats in the upright position. And no smoking.'

Tony uncoupling from Matilda, the bumping getting almost violent; it's difficult to move around, Matilda reeling, drooping into the seat she was being screwed over moments before, Frannie and Tony struggling to get their seats upright, buckling themselves in, Tony's cock glistening, still erect as the plane drops sickeningly, leaving their insides twenty feet above them and Matilda wails in fear.

The pilot's voice again. 'It feels far worse than it is, Lady Ballington. We're well clear of any potential trouble. I repeat, not the slightest thing to worry about, we'll be through it in ten, fifteen minutes maximum.'

Frannie leans forward, resting a comforting hand on Matilda's shoulder. Matilda is trembling and when she turns fear-filled eyes at Frannie, Frannie sees that her forehead is beaded with perspiration. She murmurs words of comfort, knowing that nothing will help, she's seen her like this on similar occasions before. But Frannie herself is unphased by a bit of turbulence and Tony, judging by his unflagging erection, is not too concerned either. Frannie stares at it, fascinated, it looks particularly erotic, arousing, poking up from beneath a buckled seat-belt. She takes it in her free hand, leaving the other on Matilda's shoulder, jerks her fist up and down it, feeling its heat and power and when the plane drops again, at least twenty feet, the stomach-losing is an extra kick. Bending, Tony contrives to reach her middle with his mouth; it's impossible, so instead he works two fingers between her legs and they sit there, riding the plane which bumps around like a bronco in a rodeo show, urgently tossing each other off.

The cockpit door opens, the stewardess pokes her head into the cabin to see that everyone's all right. Her eyes bulge and she mutters, 'My God,' and disappears, slamming the door. She did not get a look at what Frannie and Tony were up to, she could only see their heads and shoulders, but what she did see was shocking in its total unexpectedness; the naked Matilda, strapped into one of the front seats, a few feet from her, trembling in fear.

Frannie in yet another first-time sex situation, finding it powerfully erotic, the being strapped down, the limited possibilities of movement, the being half-clothed throwing emphasis on below-the-waist

100

nakedness, the violence of the plane. She's close to coming; so is Tony – she can feel it by the way he tenses. She speeds up the action of her fist; her other hand leaves Matilda to take hold of his balls, Tony matches her rhythm with his two probing fingers, faster now, almost there, Tony straining his middle section against the seat belt, eyes closing, back arching, a groan, and then shooting, one, two, three, four, rich, powerful spurts over the back of Matilda's seat and, moments later Frannie comes with a long, sighed, 'Ahhh', knees convulsed together, her hand still wrapped around Tony's cock. She closes her eyes for several seconds while her pulse gets itself back to normal and, when she opens them, she says, with a smile, 'No elephants, then?'

He returns the smile. 'Most definitely no elephants.'

# 8

# Twilight Zone

There was to be no more sex on that flight. Frannie and Tony managed to struggle into their clothes, which meant unbuckling and risking being thrown over, or into the roof, without serious mishap, but they took that risk because, their passion spent, sitting so blatantly exposed began to feel awkward, if not somewhat ridiculous. But Matilda, in her state of elongated fear, flew at five hundred miles an hour through the heavy weather unaware of her nakedness.

When the seat belt light went out there was no public announcement. Frannie surmised that the stewardess's revelation had rendered the pilot unsure as to how its reaction on him would affect his tone of voice. She helped the seemingly shell-shocked Matilda to get dressed. It had been Matilda's worst flying experience and she was not to recover fully until both her feet were planted on terra firma.

At tea time they were refuelling at Shannon in the Irish Republic in preparation for the last six hundred and fifty mile hop to Amsterdam, during which Frannie won three dollars from Tony playing backgammon; by early evening they were dropping down low over a choppy, ominous-looking North Sea on their approach path to Schiphol Airport.

Gregory was there waiting for them, having flown scheduled airlines throughout the night and arriving that morning. He had hired a small Mercedes, the 190, an ideal sized car for negotiating the narrow, sometimes tortuous streets of ancient colourful Amsterdam.

Frannie was booked in the one hundred and twenty year old Amstel Hotel in the heart of the city in a classic, typical European-style suite which was well matched to the mood and the façade of the hotel. When they checked in it was dark and quite chilly, but Frannie nevertheless enjoyed a whisky on her terrace which overlooked a broad expanse of the River Amstel whose lazy waters reflected the myriad coloured lights from the elegant old buildings lining its banks. Just before a bend in the river, about two hundred yards from where Frannie stood, was an ancient bridge, almost baroque in its ornamentation, a continuous string of cars and bicycles crossing it. Bicycles! Where else could she be but Amsterdam, unless it were Oxford? Enjoying the view, discovering a relaxed, heady feeling in the nippy air, Frannie felt very much a part of it; there was Dutch blood in her, a great-grandmother, three generations removed, and she understood how it was to be European, that rather special feeling of belonging to Europe as a whole. Frannie was happy with herself. For all that had happened to her on the trip so far she remained only herself, young, beautiful, unsullied, an especially privileged member of the human race who appreciated that fact.

She had agreed to let Tony take her to dinner – he insisted on saying thank you. Afterwards he took her bar-hopping in the Walletjes, the red light district, an area criss-crossed with canals and bridges, and colourful, wooden, gabled and buttressed houses many of which were two to three hundred years old. Frannie had not visited this part of the city before and, strolling with Tony through what was one of the world's famed sexual playgrounds, she was agreeably surprised to find little evidence of an undercurrent of violence, no atmosphere of menace. Here the ladies of the night sat on open display in lighted windows, many behind the little square panes of houses protected by the city council. Most of the girls were wearing some form of lingerie, many of them were young and attractive and as Frannie and Tony passed, arm-in-arm, Frannie extravagant in a full length Emba white mink coat, they tapped their windows to attract attention; those that smiled received smiles in return.

The roads by the canals were narrow and, to prevent parking on the side fronting the houses there were rows of bollards with the symbol of Amsterdam, three crosses on top of each other standing for Charitable, Courageous and Determined, painted on them. Tony pointed out how very much these posts looked like erect penises, there were endless jokes about them and Frannie, laughing, agreed, they remarkably resembled human phalli at the ready.

They crossed a bridge bearing quite heavy traffic, the fastest moving of which was the bicycles, and in among the crawling vehicles was a taxi with a freshly painted, eye-catching advert on its door. Tony pointed it out. 'That's where I shall be working,' he said. 'Casa Roso.'

Frannie looked up at him. 'I thought you said you were going to work in a live sex show? On stage?'

'That's right.'

'But – they advertise that sort of thing on taxis?'

'Why not? Don't forget this is one of the most liberated cities in the world. People come from all over to visit it, a big percentage just for the sex. The city gives them what they want, and if that's it, why not advertise it?'

'Why not indeed? I'm all for it. But I can't help comparing it with sad old London, which I adore. Soho. Sex shops abounding, but the real stuff, books you see on open display in every newsagents here, under the counter and three times the price because of it. Dirty little strip clubs where the girls have to keep still once they've got their knickers off and then the lights go out. Sleazy so-called clubs where they show really *bad* porno films and videos, terrible prints, most of them ancient.'

'You've actually been to these places yourself?'

'Of course. With my husband.'

'Isn't that a bit risky? I hear those London dives get raided all the time. Lord and Lady Ballington in police raid on porn cinema would look great in the press.'

Frannie shrugged. 'Victor wouldn't give a damn. Neither would I. I rather think our friends would find it frightfully amusing.'

Tony shook his head. 'You English. And what about those girls trying to make an honest living at the world's oldest profession, having to advertise in shop windows using *double-entendres*? French lessons, third floor, stocks and bonds, that sort of thing.'

'It all seems – is – so damned unnecessary.'

'It sure does. You know, a heck of a lot of the girls in the sex business in Amsterdam are British.'

'I'll just bet they are.' She stopped, tugging at Tony's elbow. 'Gosh, *she's* pretty.' A girl in a brightly-lit window, no more than twenty, thick, blonde hair, natural, cascading to her waist, sitting, knees neatly crossed, satin suspenders, fine blue silk stockings, diaphanous blue peignoir. She smiled, beckoning to them. Frannie smiled a sad, whimsical smile back.

'Is she not,' said Tony. 'Tell you what, I'll treat us to her if you fancy it.'

Frannie shook her head to the girl, tapping her watch, the universal gesture of no time – she did not want the girl to feel undesired – then she moved on, taking Tony with her. 'Thanks for the offer,' she said. 'Strangely enough I'm not much in the mood. We'll

105

stroll some more, have another drink perhaps, then I'm for an early night.'

'Oh.' Tony looked disappointed. 'I was kind of thinking we could get it on tonight, just the two of us.'

'Mmmm.' She stopped again, putting the end of her finger on the side of his nose. 'You have got to rest up, you have. You start work tomorrow night, remember? How many times a night was it you told me? Four?'

He grinned. 'That doesn't change anything. As a matter of fact I just wanted to see if I can still get it up in private.'

'Oh, *thanks*.'

'No, seriously, I fancy you like mad, Frannie.'

'Then you're forgiven. But I'm sorry, not tonight. Some other time, perhaps.I really *am* rather tired.'

He sighed. 'Have it your way. I'll never understand women!' They walked some way in silence until they reached a brightly lit, red-fronted theatre, where Tony stopped them. Casa Roso.

'That's it,' he said. 'That's where I work.'

Frannie peered at the photos by the door. Couples in various stages of undress, locked in sexual embraces on a stage. 'My, my,' she commentated. '*Interesting*.' She looked closer at one colour picture. A naked man, standing, being attended to by a coloured girl, also naked, on her knees. 'And that's you, of course.' She chuckled, unable to resist the comment. 'I'd know that cock anywhere!'

'Behave, for God's sake. You've already turned me down, now don't start turning me on!'

'Sorry. Naughty of me.'

'Forgiven. But don't do it again.' He paused. 'I have an idea. Why don't you come tomorrow? Take in the show. When I'm free I a can probably introduce you to one or two interesting people.'

'I don't really know about walking in a place like this alone.'

106

'A lot of people do. Women as well as men. You'd be surprised.'

'I don't think it's quite my style, Tony.'

'So, why don't you come with Matilda?'

She coughed. 'Don't you think it might be a little bad for her?'

'I think it'll be *very* bad for her.'

She thought about it. 'In that case, all right, I'll bring her!' And they both roared with laughter.

Gregory dropped them off at Casa Roso at ten the following evening, Frannie having treated Matilda to a fine meal in one of her favourite Amsterdam restaurants, the unpromisingly named Five Flies.

As he drew up outside the garish exterior, Gregory frowned disapproval at it. 'I don't think this can be the place, Lady Ballington,' he said. 'There must be two of them.'

But Frannie was already opening her door. 'No, this is it. Come on, Matilda.' And they were out before Gregory had time to assist them. A wicked moment visiting her, Frannie rapped on Gregory's side window and he let it down. 'You'll probably have to drive around a few times before you find a parking space nearby,' she said. 'When you've got one take a look at the pictures over there. I think you'll find you'll recognize one of them.' Taking Matilda's arm, she led her to the door where she paused, drawing attention to the photo of Tony with the black girl.

'Oh dear,' was Matilda's comment. 'You really shouldn't be so forward with Gregory. You know how he is, you'll upset him for sure.'

'I know. But Amsterdam, my dear, seems to have put me in that sort of mood. Anyway, he shouldn't be such a fuddy-duddy.' She searched in her handbag for money, which she kept in chaotic, crumpled balls. 'And you know, he *still* has the nerve to treat me to that occasional, you-know-what look!'

Matilda snorted. 'Which you encourage.'

'Do I?' She straightened out some notes. 'This *is* Dutch money, isn't it?'

Casa Roso turned out to be a plush, over-decorated, over-lit theatre with some two hundred seats in tiers sloping down to a smallish stage. It was more than half-full when they went in, the audience quite mixed, and Frannie was surprised to observe a number of perfectly ordinary, respectable-looking couples in its midst.

They selected two seats near the middle and Frannie parked next to the male half of one of those unexceptional duos, Dutch from the top of his neatly barbered, stubborn head to the tip of his sensible, thick-soled brogues. Her entrance, in a figure-clinging, black lace chiffon dress by Richat Chaléard, her blonde tresses gleaming and falling free, caused a minor stir amongst those in close vicinity, even the impassive Dutchman sneaking her an admiring glance which was curtailed by his wife.

Once they were comfortable, Frannie and Matilda noticed a marked difference between the comportment of this waiting audience compared to that of the usual theatre crowd. There was a hushed expectancy in the air of the kind which hits a theatre audience only when the lights begin to dim; but there was no indication at that moment that this particular show was about to begin. Frank Sinatra, on tape, was Doing It His Way, and a lady clad in a tightly-laced corset, huge breasts straining, threatening to erupt over the top, with black high heels with matching net stockings and her dyed hair piled high above an overly made-up face was doing it hers, acting in what appeared, to Frannie and Matilda, a most extraordinary manner. As a steady stream of people trickled in this lady danced slowly in the aisle, in time to Sinatra, and whenever a man on his own, or two, or a group of males arrived, she would swoop her hand forward, a sudden dive like an eagle going for a rabbit, and grab one or other of them firmly between the legs. Yet this eccentric, management-inspired behaviour, which would no doubt, had it been permissable, have had the audience of a London vaudeville show in hysterics, here was eliciting merely mild amusement, and the unwitting victims usually accepted this sexual assault with either a flinch followed by a self-conscious grin, or a good-natured oath.

Frannie observed this performance in astonishment, eyes wide and chin lifting in a little jerk each time a man was handled like that. After a while, she said to Matilda, 'What on earth is that all about?'

'I must say it's very odd, isn't it?' Then she gasped. 'Dear God, will you look at that!' A sailor, wearing the uniform of the French Navy, had stopped as he was pounced on and grabbed her firmly between her legs in return and, as his hand was pulled away, he put both hands on her shoulders and, laughing, got her down on her knees in front of him, where he slid down his zipper. Going along with the game part of the way, she slipped her hand inside his trousers and then withdrew it, empty, gazing at her palm in mock surprise, then she stood and playfully slapped his cheeks and the whole performance, including the sailor's rolled eyes and his loud, 'mon Dieu!', brought the loudest laughs of this curious pre-show ritual.

The lights faded, coloured spots hit the stage, the music changed to the very slow 'Sally' by Sade, and a blonde woman in her early thirties wearing a full-length coat of an indistinguishable grey fur gyrated on-stage where she began slowly removing her below-the-waist apparel while the spots slid through the spectrum on her. Her dancing was just short of clumsy, and she contrived not to appear bored. Down to lace panties, she unbuttoned her blouse letting well-hung breasts swing free and exhibited them to the audience, her hands cupping them from underneath, pushing them forward, offering them. Then, turning her back, she stepped out of her panties, dropped to her knees with her legs slightly apart, bending forward with her weight resting on one hand whilst with the other she drew the heavy material of the fur coat up her thighs until it rested piled high on her back, staying like that for long seconds, rocking slowly just through no more than three inches, in time to 'Sally'. The rhythm of the sensuous rocking unchanged, she opened herself up with two fingers and the blatant exposure reminded Frannie of that night in New York kneeling over the bean-bag and the memory, rather than the sexual performance, began to rouse her.

The woman then put herself through the exhibition scenes which are standard fair in live sex shows, masturbating, introducing a banana in herself, a candle a vibrator, never removing the coat, then she finally faked orgasm and left the stage to mild applause.

A white spotlight hovered over the starkly empty platform, looking for a reason to be there and, turning her head, Frannie peered up to locate the source. There was a mezzanine where an array of spotlights bordered a bar overlooking the theatre. Nudging Matilda, Frannie said, 'There's Tony.'

'Where?'

'Upstairs doing the lights.'

Matilda spotted him. 'Strange. Is *that* all he ...?' But her unfinished question was answered as the woman from the first set, minus the fur but wearing the same skirt and blouse which had been discarded on stage, took over control of the lights from Tony and he vanished.

'I *see*.' Frannie smiled inwardly. 'The Dutch

110

mentality, of course. Waste no chance of saving money.'

On stage, an odd scene was beginning to unfold. A thick-set man in a leather mask, his body criss-crossed with heavy leather straps, wearing multi-studded and zippered leather underpants, a heavy leather collar around his neck is brought, on a lead, into the spotlight by a lady who is supposed to look wicked, the surrounds of her eyes painted with thick, emerald green make-up reaching into sharp points high on her temples. She is dressed in a leather pants suit which has holes cut out for her rouged nipples, and their surrounds, to protrude through; it has no crotch-piece in the pants, leaving her sexual parts naked, but suggestively framed. The music changing now, an increase in tempo, 'Smooth Operator', as the lights begin their spectrum sliding, the 'slave' gets on hands and knees and his 'mistress' rides him around the stage. Frannie and Matilda greatly amused, neither one of them finding the show so far particularly erotic, but the action begins to warm up, and by the time the man has his hands tied behind him with the dog's lead his pants unzipped and his erect member in the woman's mouth, they are both becoming mildly aroused although leather itself and the somewhat gross flavour of the contrived sado-masochistic scenes – in which no one actually gets beaten – adds nothing to the sexual interest of publicly-displayed fellatio for them.

Act follows act, the participants each having their turns at the lights and, presumably, the music. Never the last word in erotisism, Frannie decides, a mildish turn-on only, there is something about the quite unattractive stage, the accompanying music, always in the same vein, always Sade, by now monotonous to her ear, the being a part of a large audience, which taints the enjoyment of performances, some of which, under different, more intimate circumstances, might have proved to be big turn-ons.

Then, 'Hang on to Your Love', the surprise of watching a woman being steadily buggered by a young black stud, somehow she had not thought they would go quite *that* far, and the even greater surprise of suddenly noticing that the middle-aged hand belonging to the wife of the ruddy-faced, respectable Dutch burgher on her left has found its way inside half-unzippered cream slacks and moves unobtrusively, but steadily. At once she finds this more interesting, more erotic, than anything happening on stage and her eyes, two peeping toms continually flicker sideways to linger on this unexpected sight, though she is very careful to keep her face facing front.

Tony appears on stage with two women. They're all quickly naked and he's giving all he's capable of, reminding Frannie vividly of being screwed by him on camera, and of her brief episode of him having Matilda over the seat at twenty-nine thousand feet. Suddenly, she's turned on, getting wet as the Dutch wife's hand moves a little more obviously and Tony's heavy action speeds up. The stoic Dutch features of the man by her have gone tense except for a twitching jaw muscle; he seems to be pressing his back hard against the chair and Frannie thinks, to hell with it, if this farmer can enjoy that sort of thing so can she, and she leads Matilda's hand under her skirt. The Dutchman comes with an almost inaudible hiss of breath sucked through clenched teeth, eyes glazing, he no longer sees the stage where Tony has two avid mouths working on him, the tip of his cock going from one to the other; he's on a couch, legs splayed, girls kneeling on either side of him, an almost white spot clearly picking out the action.

Frannie wondering just how much cum the Dutchman's orgasm has released, by his expression it's no more than half a drip, but perhaps his pants are *soaked*, as she steadily opens and closes her thighs against Matilda's hand, Matilda's fingers working with great assurance and enthusiasm, she knows exactly how her mistress should be tended to.

Tony, coming, directing the first spurt over the face of one girl, a second into the other's mouth, then spraying the rest over the first girl's tits and leaning back, closing his eyes, still holding onto himself as the lights go out and Frannie climaxes quietly with a long drawn out sigh.

The house lights came on. It was suddenly, shockingly, bright, the audience unnaturally quiet. The Dutchman had not moved, he was sitting very upright, facing front.

Matilda whispered, with a little giggle, 'Fine state you've left *me* in!'

'Sorry.' Frannie arranged a lock of hair over her breast. 'I really didn't expect anything like that was going to happen to me.'

'Your neighbours have something to do with it?'

'Oh, you saw it too?'

'Not half.'

'It had a weird reaction on me. Two old farts like that, yet it turned the trick faster than anything down there could ever have done.'

The 'old farts' were getting up, Frannie's perverse eyes sought a damp patch on his trousers but found nothing. They began to leave, turning their backs on Frannie as Tony suddenly appeared, from the other side.

'Good heavens!' Frannie exclaimed. 'How did *you* get here so quickly?' Tony was neatly dressed in a navy blue blazer and a tie. He grinned.

'You have to be fast in this business. There's a half hour interval, I saved us a table in the bar.'

Frannie raised an eyebrow. 'Should we be seen in

the bar with you?'

'I don't see why not. Since you're in this sort of a world in any case.'

'That's one answer. Well, since we are ...' Frannie got up.

He had reserved a corner table at the rails overlooking the entire theatre, and Frannie turned heads all the way to it. As they took their places, Tony remarked, 'I bet you're the most beautiful woman who's ever been in here.'

She laughed. 'Thanks. But are you sure they're not looking at you? Curiosity?'

'No. Funny that, I seldom get recognized with my pants on.'

Matilda had stowed her glasses in her bag. She was wearing an antique, aquamarine, fine velvet dress, pearls for buttons, her hair swept up in classic Hellenic style and the way she had presented herself that evening complimented Frannie's beauty, but to a degree in which she didn't actually fade away, as so often, beside her mistress. She remarked, jollily, after ordering herself a Bloody Mary, 'I say, what a *show*! Bit different, I must say that.'

Frannie said, 'Yes. I don't see quite how you, um, manage to perform in front of all those people, Tony.'

'I don't see them. I pretend they're not there.'

'I see. And then, one presumes, to make sure your performance extends to the correct, ah, length, you pretend that elephants are. Or pigs, whatever. What an extraordinarily athletic brain you do have!'

They all laughed, Matilda, having been, enlightened over dinner about the esoteric elephants, the loudest. Then Tony said, 'It's not all that difficult, you know.'

'But *four* times a night?' Frannie, in mock-admiration.

Matilda was feeling at her most daring. 'I fail to see how you can have anything, you know, left at the end of the night. Even supposing you continue to rise to the occasion.'

'I can get it up all right. And what happens is this ...'
An explanation was denied to them as two men approached the table and Tony got to his feet. The men were impeccably dressed, one, who appeared to be about fifty was tall, slim with slicked-back thinning hair and with the sort of aquiline nose which suggests asthetisism. He was wearing a double-breasted maroon pin-striped suit with a club tie and crocodile shoes. The other, some fifteen years younger, half a head shorter, was prematurely grey, but it suited his regular features, and he wore a smart grey leather jacket over fashion trousers which peg-topped grey suede boots. Frannie thought the two of them fractionally over-adorned, gold watch, wrist chain and ring wise, but that it was not enough to offend. Tony said, 'Good evening, Mr Prinsen, Danny.'

The older man said, 'Hi Tony. There was no other place to sit. I wonder, could we impose ourselves?' He was looking, not at the two empty chairs, but at Frannie.

'Of course.' Tony made the introductions and the two men sat down. Jan Prinsen, the older man, it appeared was the owner of a similar club where Tony sometimes managed to squeeze in a bit of extra work, and Danny, whose other name Frannie had failed to catch was a close friend of his from London with some sort of allied, permanent business in Amsterdam. Both men took an immediate obvious interest in Frannie and, to a lesser, and probably only polite extent, in Matilda who had sacrificed vanity for vision by replacing her bi-focals. When Tony left to prepare something to do with the lights, Prinsen ordered champagne and they were joined by a third man, Willem, under thirty, who was possessed of a smile to trap flashbulbs and a sense of humour broad enough

115

to match. He sat next to Matilda who, clearly captivated by him from the off, very quickly made the reverse sacrifice with her spectacles.

By the time the beginning of the second half of the show approached the conversation at their table had split into two sections; Frannie and her two friends on the one hand and Matilda and Willem on the other. Prinsen and Danny were paying Frannie elaborate attention and she found them rather intriguing: they were both attractive in their way and terribly self-assured, still there was something about them which she could not fathom, second selves lingering beneath the surface; the extended diphong manner of speech of the Londoner might have carried a hint of femininity about it, the Dutchman's way of sliding the occasional sidelong glance at him whilst talking to Frannie, as if seeking approval, she found a touch strange.

The five elected to watch the show from where they were. It turned out to be little more than variations of the first half, the same performers in different costumes, when they wore anything at all; there was one innovative scene involving skateboards, but Frannie's personal experience was so much beyond what was happening down there that by then she failed to find it little more than an amusing diversion, hardly erotic at all. But there was an innate eroticism in the air which overrode any slight sexual stirrings over the stage, embodied in the fact of sitting with male strangers, watching with them people coupling on stage whilst being aware that the attention of two of them was more on her than on the performance; so potent was her awareness of this that she could almost feel them imagining doing to her what was being done on stage.

Matilda, meanwhile, to Frannie's amused delight, had the undivided attention of the young Dutchman

Willem whose arm had stolen around her plump waist and who occasionaly treated her ear to an unresisted, tongue-intruding kiss, making her wriggle.

After the show, in the ladies' room, Frannie remarked with, mock-disapproval, 'You're coming on a bit strong with Willem, aren't you?'

Matilda was carefully preening herself in an ornate, gilt-framed mirror, paying more than usual attention to her make-up. Without her spectacles she had to lean so that her nose was less than a foot from the glass in order to get herself in focus. Re-touching a fine black line at the corner of an eye, she said, 'I think we've pretty well got a tacit agreement to go off together later. Do you um, do you mind?'

'Mind? Why on earth should I mind? He seems a nice enough boy. Do you the world of good, shouldn't wonder.'

'I don't know if I should leave you with those two men.'

'What are you talking about? Why the hell not?' Straightening a stocking seam.

'They're being very intense about you, I'd say. Too much so.'

'Oh yes? And what's sticking your tongue in the ear of someone you've known for little more than half an hour being?'

'That's not what I meant. That happens to be one of those rare occurences that feel absolutely right. Those fellows, that Jan and Danny, there's something not quite normal – over the top if you know what I mean – about the way they've been concentrating on you. Like, they're absolutely determined to get something together, maybe something kinky; they don't want to miss a trick in their approach to you.'

'Mmm. Well, a threesome, no doubt.' She inspected her hair, turning this way and that. 'I might even like that, this place has put me in that sort of mood. I can handle it. There is one thing, though. I do get the strangest of feelings that Danny may be gay.'

'There you are, you see. I'd say there's far more to those two than meets the eye.'

Frannie smiled, her face sharing unconcerned amusement. 'It looks as if I'm going to find out, doesn't it? In any case, should anything untoward happen, there's always the good Gregory.'

Midnight. Frannie in the back of the Mercedes 190 as the 'good' but subdued Gregory followed the tail lights of a white Rolls with Jan Prinsen driving, Danny at his side, over a little humped-back bridge and then left to follow the banks of yet another canal. The traffic was thin now that they were out of the Walletjes, even the bicycles had virtually disappeared. Matilda had departed the Casa Roso half an hour previously with her Dutch boy, no Gregory to protect her but Frannie was convinced that with that clean young man no rescue would be called for – if anybody would need it it would be him!

On the other hand she was nursing the faintest suspicion about the two in the Rolls ahead of them. By the time they had left the theatre her feeling that Danny might be gay, that he swung both ways, had increased and it followed that if he did then most probably his friend did also, though Prinsen had given no indication of it. But this possibility was by no means making her consider calling off this new adventure; the combined effects of the evening had made her horny enough to already have them mentally with their pants down.

She suddenly remembered her special bag, tucked away in a cupboard in the back of Gregory's seat, and, taking it out, she clipped a new film into place and transferred the contents of her black velvet evening bag into it. Whatever transpired on this chilly

Amsterdam night, she would put on record for the later enjoyment of her voyeuristic husband.

They were driving along a gentle curve in the banks of the Singel canal when the Rolls pulled through the gates of a large, end terrace house, looking at least as old and as well preserved as any in the city, and stopped in front of a garage. There was room for the Mercedes, and the heavily silent Gregory pulled up alongside the Rolls, got out and opened her door, treating her to a stony-faced touch of his cap as he did so, his facetious display of disapproval causing her a minor stab of irritation. But as soon as she found herself inside the house the moment was forgotten.

They went into a hallway where nothing was quite straight, walls, ceiling or floor, yet all hung together in charming harmony. The doors were of intricately carved oak, the low ceiling supported by slender, warped beams, a very narrow staircase with an ornate balustrade led up into darkness. It was warm, but there was no physical evidence of central heating. Prinsen led the way into a spacious room which was a logical extension of the hallway, with diamond-shaped, leaded windows on two adjacent walls; curiously, Frannie was reminded of the windows of the porn magazine proprietor's house in Florida, copy of this very same style. The Dutchman switched on lights and closed heavy green velvet curtains. Frannie caught a glimpse of a baleful Gregory staring in at them from behind the wheel of his car before the last one shut.

As her eyes examined the room – generous armchairs and a broad sofa in velvet to match the curtains, the rest of the furniture delicate, spindly woodwork of a period unfamiliar with her but superbly in keeping with the age of the house, bright, gold-framed landscape paintings on oak-panelled walls, a flattering portrait of Jan Prinsen himself over a

carved stone fireplace in which no fire was needed –
Frannie remarked, 'My chauffeur doesn't appear to
approve of tonight.' Casually, she placed her bag on a
bookshelf, the lens pointing towards the sofa and,
taking a pack of cigarettes from within, she activated
the film mechanism.

Prinsen had slid aside a wall panel, revealing a well-
stocked bar and a small fridge. He said, 'And are you
caring what your chauffeur thinks?'

She lit a cigarette. 'Of course not. But he nevertheless
succeeds in making me feel a touch awkward. Ridiculous, I know.'

'Perhaps you are liking each other too much?'
Innuendo, which she chose to ignore. He opened the
fridge. 'Shall we continue with champagne?'

'Why not?' She puffed the cigarette once more, then
stubbed it out; it did not taste right, had in any case only
been an excuse to start the camera.

'Make mine a scotch, Jan,' Danny said. He was staring intently at Frannie with the palest of cold blue eyes,
eyes which suggested Nordic blood in his veins, and
Frannie, not unwilling for things to start quickly – that
was, after all, her reason for being here – stared cooly
back, her dimple puckering as she smiled her smallest
smile. Prinsen was easing the cork from a bottle of Krug
when Danny, no more words, reached for her, pulling
her into his arms and kissing her, but clumsily, a first
kiss which had nothing to do with the stirrings of love,
as his hands slid down the black lace of her dress and
tightened themselves on the flesh of her buttocks. She
pressed mechanically against him, forcing herself into a
response which was a little too early, hearing the champagne cork pop and Prinsen saying, 'Hey, you are
starting without me,' as Danny's fingers found their
way momentarily into her anal cleft before he let her go.

'Just a sample,' said Danny, eyeing her insinuatingly.
'Delights to come. *Very* nice.' He fetched her a glass of

champagne, a hefty, neat scotch in a highball glass in his other hand.

Prinsen opened another panel. TV, sound equipment, the electronic works. 'I thought to watch a video together,' he said. 'Perhaps to set a certain mood. I have a new one, from France. Very … sexy. You two, why don't you sit?' He indicated the sofa and they sunk into it side by side where Danny's hand immediately found the flesh of Frannie's lace thigh, but she was still not ready, not relaxed enough in this new setting, despite her eagerness when following behind the Rolls. She had been drinking very conservatively all evening; now she needed to get a little high. Draining her champagne, she looked at Danny's glass. 'I could really do with one of those,' she said.

Danny obliged, saying, as he brought her a whisky as big as his own, 'I'm afraid Jan's all out of coke. I should have thought to ask at the club. That's what you really need, a nice line of the purest.'

'No, that's fine. I'm not at all into drugs.' She laughed drily. 'About the only vice I don't have, I imagine.'

'Why *not*? You get a fantastic high from good coke.'

'My inner resources are fairly complete.' As she made the remark it sounded a shade pompous to her. She did not elaborate, but took a long sip of the whisky, slow enough so that she would not cough on it, enjoying the feel of its heat as it punched her in the stomach, knowing from experience that two more similar slugs of the neat liquor would find themselves very quickly to her brain and produce for her the touch of euphoria which she felt she needed before throwing her body into whatever was about to happen to it.

The room was equipped with dimmer switches, the lights softened and the TV screen flickered into life, somewhere in the middle of a video. Prinsen made himself comfortable on Frannie's free side.

On screen, characters in the uniform of French prison

121

officers, two men, one woman, were interrogating a female prisoner. They were acting very angry and twice the prisoner was slapped around the face.

Danny said, 'Do you speak French?'

'Not really.' The third slug of scotch inside her, that good, warm glow was spreading through her, the lines of the room going slightly fuzzy as if the lights had been dimmed even more and she settled back to enjoy whatever was coming up on the screen.

'Neither do I, but with this sort of movie it really doesn't matter.' Danny's hand found her thigh once more and this time it was welcomed by a closing of her legs.

'I shouldn't think it does,' she murmured.

*CUT TO: The prisoner, dragged into a cell by the two male warders, struggling . as she is stripped naked, being handcuffed to a ring high up in the cell wall. Angry interrogation, threatenings with a riding crop, sobs, negative shakes of her head.*

(Frannie, leaning forward, cupping her chin in hand, intrigued at first, a little beating, just so that it stings and smarts, the exposure of naked parts to belt or cane or crop always a turn-on. But then flickers of doubt, touches of fear, because the crop begins to cut into the on-screen girl's flesh, it draws blood and, as it does so, each time it stripes her, Frannie grips her chin a little harder but Danny's hand on her thigh convulses.)

*NEW SHOT: The prisoner, sobbing, released from the ring.*

*TRACKING THE THREE OF THEM: The Naked Prisoner, a warder, at each elbow, fighting against them, being conducted through two rows of cells, curious female faces at the bars, some of them jeering.*

*CUT TO: The interior of another cell, a large bunk, the*

*Prisoner being dragged to it, forced face down on it, while one warder goes to her head, undoes his trousers, takes out his erect cock and forces it between her lips, laughing.*

(Frannie's little touch of fear passes, she likes this, it's already better than anything live on stage with an audience of two hundred. She leans back and Prinsen's hand slides into the top of her dress, gentle fingers find their way under her bra, pinching her nipples. Danny's hand, still on the outside of her dress, is pushing its way deeper into her crotch and she facilitates it by parting her knees the four inches or so the skirt will allow. Immersed now in two separate sexual impressions now, two experiences, the events on screen and what is happening to her combining to accelerate a powerful need. She hoists her haunches to help Danny in easing her dress up over her hips, sinks momentarily as Danny's hand finds it way inside her mousseline knickers then lifts herself again so that he can slide them down her thighs as Prinsen, managing the catch at the back of the neck of her dress, unzips it, the sound of the zipper as small and precise and as gut-catching to Frannie's ears as that moment of sound in *Last Tango in Paris* when Marlon Brando rips Maria Schneider's panties before fucking her standing up. She hunches her shoulders to help him move the dress forwards and it falls to join the heap of the rest of itself at her waist.)

*TIGHT ON THE CELL GROUP. The Prisoner letting herself go now, cock-sucking with evident mounting enjoyment.*

(Frannie's bra is off and Prinsen, mouth at her neck, little nips with his teeth, has an arm around her back and both elbows on either side of her waist as he cups and fondles her willing, erect-nippled breasts. Danny has two fingers working inside her, she rocks on the sofa against them, knees opening and closing, eyes watching every movement on the screen.)

*CLOSE-UP: A cock, sperm spurting into the prisoner's mouth, over her face.*

(Frannie unzips Prinsen's flies, finds his erection, pulls the head of it out over the top of his pants. Prinsen, uncupping one breast, reaches down and ... undoes Danny's trousers. But Frannie misses this little manoeuvre because exactly one half of her is still engrossed in the video. Mewling along with the orgasms, getting Prinsen's member clear of his underpants, hooking the elastic under his balls, squeezing him, Frannie reaches a blind hand to Danny's flies where she encounters a fisted cock. She looks. It is not Danny's hand, but Prinsen's. Prinsen is slowly masturbating his friend.)

Credits began to move down the screen as Frannie was struck with the powerful realization that, here, she was getting herself into far more than she had bargained for. Shocked, she was nevertheless too far down the heady road of lust for the fact of a homosexual act taking place in their threesome to dampen her enthusiasm. Danny's fingers were busy inside her with the same insistence with which Prinsen's hand jerked his cock and, as the intensity of movement increased, as one man's lust for his friend communicated itself through his friend's fingers to Frannie's cunt so her hand, a life of its own, found the same rhythm on Prinsen's swollen member and all three of them got lost in the depths of differing, urgent, sexual needs, Danny's hot mouth feeding off her spare breast and Prinsen's tongue wet inside her ear. The TV screen a crackle of static, Frannie's exterior centre of attention shifted inevitably to her first sight of one man's hand stimulating another man's penis; she became riveted by it, finding that it added fuel to her sexual fire, another weird new turn-on and that, and Danny's fingers up her, and the feel of Prinsen's big cock in her hand, the shared vibrations, combined to be too much for her, her buttocks tensed away from the soft velvet of the sofa, her thighs gripping Danny's knuckles with a primordial power as she voiced her orgasm with a groan which shuddered.

But the climax did no more for her than to assuage her immediate needs; there was no libidinal climb-down and moments later she slipped to the floor, to her knees, removing both men's shoes, then their socks, deliberate about it, dragging their trousers and underpants down and off, stealing glances at them as she did so, as they moved close together on the sofa, as Danny's hand took a hold of Prinsen's cock and they worked at each other in unison. Squatting there, watching them with her face on a level with their mid-sections, Frannie became consumed with an awful fascination, hypnotised by the sight of two men like that and, as their mouths came together above her, her hand found its way to the wetness between her legs.

Prinsen and Danny break off their homosexual mingling of mouths and their mutual masturbation comes almost, but not quite, to a halt as, one thought in both minds they stare at Frannie, the power of their lascivious urges contriving to contort their expressions to the extent they have become almost frighteningly different and Frannie shivers with a mingling of dread and her own powerful lust.

Prinsen says, a tremor in his voice, 'You fancy something very special, Frannie?'

She swallows. 'I thought you guys didn't need me any more.'

125

'*Au contraire*. It sweetens the pleasure.'

'All right.' A feeling of smallness. And excitement.

Prinsen getting up, moving a coffee table behind the sofa, taking Frannie's elbow, helping her to her feet, stripping her dress off, over her head, dropping it on the floor, getting Frannie to her knees again, but this time on the sofa, straddling Danny, her cunt pushed into his face, having her bend across the sofa back and rest her weight on her hands on the coffee table. Danny's tongue, finding its way inside her, fucking her with it as, biting her lower lip, moving slowly against the little prick-tongue, she sees Prinsen leaving the room and, moments later returning, naked now, his shirt and tie left behind somewhere, his cock still hard, carrying something which he makes a show of exhibiting to her as he passes her face: a clear plastic bottle of Johnson's Baby oil. She understands, her sphincter contracts in an anticipation which is exquisite. There are no porno directors' 'by your leaves?' here, he gets behind her, lubricates what must be his favourite hole then, infinitely carefully, he eases into her, taking it one small step at a time, first just the head of his cock, in and out with that, then each little thrust a fraction of an inch deeper, in-out, in-out, driving her to giddy heights as that thick shaft works its way further up her arse, a steady, insistent rhythm counterpointed by Danny's tongue which pokes and stabs up her cunt as far as he can reach it. The fires beginning to consume her now, Frannie takes one hand from the coffee table and sucks her thumb, imagining yet another cock, then she reaches back and between her legs, groping for Prinsen's balls, she wants to feel his balls, and she finds another hand there, busy – Danny's who is immersed in two distinct pleasures.

Frannie is close once again to climax, and Prinsen unplugs her, takes her by the shoulders and has her turn around and lay back into the sofa, the cheeks of her arse on the edge, her feet on the floor, legs wide apart. The two men take their places in this new tableau with no exchange of words, they've been this route before. Danny, who still wears a shirt, kneels on the floor between her legs, going back to his tongue work, one hand under her buttocks and middle finger probing where Prinsen's cock had just left, the other hand kneeding her breasts, the tit, massage and tongue work speeding up as Prinsen pushes Danny's shirt high up his back, oils his passage, kneels behind him and slips in his cock. Perhaps Frannie has never *felt* thoroughly lewd before this moment, this involvment in a homosexual scene brings out her dirtiest inner feelings as she watches, enrapt, not daring to believe the extent of her fascination, her view of the top of a head between her thighs, Prinsen, from the muscular belly up, facing her, hands gripping Danny's hips, eyes closed as he does to Danny what he had been doing to Frannie, almost the whole length of that cock in and out between Danny's buttocks. It does not last long, the sinews of his neck strain, his thrusts become urgent, grunting jerks and his final lunge rams Danny's head even deeper into her crotch and then he keeps perfectly still except for the muscular reaction of his seed pumping into his friend.

Danny does not move for long moments, either, and Frannie, her thighs taut and aching with need wonders if he has come too but, slowly, his head comes up, the eyes half closed yet piercingly cold as he looks at her and says, the words coming chillingly flat, 'You want a really good, powerful fucking? In that sweet cunt of yours?' And she voices no reply but her expression says all and Danny lays her on her back on the sofa and gives her just that, and gives it and gives it and *gives* it until she shouts out her orgasm; then Danny straddles her belly and Prinsen tosses him off over her tits, a warm flood which Danny smears across her skin with both hands, massaging it into her as the Dutchman, a peculiar light in his eyes, says, 'Merely for hors d'oeuvres, my dear.'

Frannie, eyes closed, breathing deeply, body awash in sexual afterglow, feeling magnificently soiled, fails to ponder the significance of these words. Danny unclips her suspender belt, pulls the stockings down and over her feet without bothering to unfasten the suspenders, and throws them on top of her dress.

She heard Prinsen pouring fresh drinks, the chinking of ice cubes and, her heartbeat more or less back to normal, she opened her eyes as a glass was thrust into her hand. More whisky. His cock hung limp above her as he said, over the rim of a champagne glass, 'Then you are liking our little sexual variations?'

Frannie eyed his equipment. 'Apparently I do, yes.' A quick inner examination found her unrepentant of what she knew had been a thoroughly perverse enjoyment. 'Pretty obvious, wasn't it?' She sat up and tried the whisky. Now it tasted raw and she did not like the way it burnt her throat, which was a little parched. 'Can I have champagne?'

'I'll get it.' Danny's tight buttocks were starkly white in the dim light as he crossed to the bar and Frannie, knowing a little of what he must be feeling in that region, but not all, owing to the female absence of a prostate, contemplated them with more than her usual interest. Of all the heavy sex she had been involved with over the years, his was the first male arse she had seen penetrated by a cock. And she had feasted dissolutely on the sight!

Danny brought the champagne and she quickly downed the glass; it was semi-sweet, light, immensely refreshing. She handed him the glass for a refill, not particularly needing more but wanting to study his bare arse some more.

128

Prinsen perched himself on the arm of the sofa, draping an arm across her shoulders and kissing her on top of her head. 'We have other variations,' he said, mouthing a smile which was bordering on evil and which she caught because she looked up at him as he did. 'Even more interesting.'

Frannie's heart missed the proverbial beat. Danny was back with more champagne and he stood in front of her as he handed it to her, so that in her direct field of vision there were now two flaccid male organs. She sipped. 'Oh.'

'Are you game, my dear?' Prinsen stroked her hair. Game? What was this now? She said nothing, terribly aware of the two cocks, hearing in the unnatural softness of Prinsen's words an uncategorisable something which might have been hidden menace.

'Of course she's game. The British upper classes are game for anything. Aren't they, Fran?'

She managed a smile which she did not feel. And a reply. 'We didn't exactly invent sex, you know.'

Danny moved his lips close to her ear. 'Perhaps not. But isn't a little light corporal punishment known as the English vice?'

She tensed. A hollow feeling invaded her stomach. 'Is it?' Voice very small.

'I have heard that, too.' Prinsen paused, still stroking her hair, very gently, a man petting his thoroughbred cat. In that same syrupy voice he went on, 'I have a special room, a playroom, if you like. Some very amusing diversions. Would you like to see it? It's upstairs.'

An alarm bell sounded in Frannie's head. But only a very small one because she was also confronted with the sexual organs of two naked men of whom she knew she wanted more. She said, 'I think I'd rather not. We, uh, seem to be getting everything we want right here.' Her glance went from cock to cock, then from eyes to eyes. Both male faces were impassive. 'Don't we?'

'Perhaps not quite. There could be, shall we say, an added, dimension?' Prinsen stooped and kissed her ear. 'I'd love you to come upstairs. It is a very special room I assure you. You will adore it. No harm, I promise, but a big turn-on.'

'An even greater degree of stimulation,' added Danny.

Moments later Frannie, curious, seeds of fear close to taking root, yet somehow remembering her camera-bag, found herself between the two men, Danny's white rear end leading the way, Prinsen behind her, being escorted up that very narrow staircase.

As soon as she saw the room Frannie shrunk from it. It was a smallish bedroom, bathed in red light, the units concealed. Two of the walls forming one corner were mirrored, a third had several rings and hooks embedded in it and, hanging from the hooks an assortment of instruments whose intended use was obvious; bamboo canes of various lengths and thicknesses, leather belts, rubber thongs, a whip, a riding crop, two paddle-tennis bats perforated with holes. In the corner where the mirrors met there was a single mattress covered with a purple satin sheet on a gilt-plated iron bedstead with leather loops fixed to all four corners. A four-legged chrome table with a padded leather top and loose straps on the legs sat near closed orange curtains, a wardrobe had its door open revealing a row of leather and rubber garments.

'I ... rather ... don't ... think ... so,' Frannie said, her eyes wide, the flats of her hands up in front of her face as if trying to push away the image of the room, but Prinsen, behind her, hands on her arse, urged her a little step forward and clicked the door closed.

'Don't worry, Frannie,' said the Dutchman, with

false bonhomie. 'You must trust me, we are not doing anything actually violent here. It is all for fun. Make-believe. You will enjoy it, you will see. You have not yet reached your true limits. Let me put on some music.'

Sexual desire a hollow memory – it had drained out of her the instant she saw and understood the room – Frannie dropped her bag and sat on the backs of her hands on the bed. 'I, I'm afraid that this sort of thing does nothing for me,' she ventured. Then added, softly, 'I'm sorry.'

'So, you've never been spanked, you've never indulged in a spot of spanking yourself?' said Danny.

'That's hardly the point.'

'So you have then, you admit it?'

'Well, yes. Yes, I have.'

'Sure you have. And I'd bet money you love it.'

The voice of Elton John filled the room, taking a slight edge off the coldness. 'So what if I do?' she said quietly. 'There's never been any need for special … for …' she glanced around, examining the various objects with a little frown. 'For … for things like this.'

'No?' Danny selected a thin bamboo cane and flexed it. 'You've never indulged in one of these?' He put it back, unhooked a narrow leather belt. 'Or something like this?' A gleam of the promise of what was to come visited his eyes. They narrowed.

'Perhaps I have, yes. But it's still not the point. I …'

'You nothing.' He interrupted her. 'You know the game, you've played it. But you haven't ventured properly into the field before. This is it.'

'I don't know, I …'

'Look,' said Prinsen. 'We won't touch you if you don't want, okay? Not a finger. You do to us, that's all.'

Frannie shrugged, looked down at the floor. This was one situation that was not getting through to her. 'What do you want me to do?' she murmured, regretting it.

She watched, it was like being in the audience for one

131

of the stranger acts at Casa Roso, as Prinsen selected a
T-shirt like garment from the wardrobe, made of fine
rubber and pulled it over his head, then buckled a
wide rubber belt with chrome studs on it low over his
hips. He completed the outfit with a matching
headsman style mask which covered his cheeks and
stopped at the bottom of his nose; it had small slits for
eye-holes, his appearance, his genitals hanging loose
below the belt, took on an appearance approaching the
grotesque. Danny meanwhile had climbed into a
leather cat-suit affair whose trousers had an open
crotch, and put on a highwayman mask, his dressing
like that, the anticipation, clearly exciting him because
he was getting another hard-on. Elton John sung 'Cage
the Songbird' as Frannie dumbly watched the two
men. Once again she felt in the land of Kafka, nervous
and disorientated.

'Here.' Danny thrusting a garment at her, an
old-fashioned, black, whale-boned corset and she
shakes her head but he is insistent. 'Come on, it's only
a game.' And, trying to blank out her mind she finds
herself standing, allowing him to hook her into the
thing. 'Oh,' he says, 'Just one final touch,' And from
the wardrobe he produces the highest pair of
spike-heeled shoes she has ever seen. 'They ought to
be about your size.'

She climbs up into the shoes – they're too tight but
bearable – then catches sight of the three of them
reflected in the mirror in front of her. She turns her
head, there they are again from the side, and, in the
corner where the mirrors meet, there is a third image,
half in each glass; nine extremely strangely-clad
human beings, twelve counting the reality, and time
appears to slow as Frannie watches Prinsen doubling
his body over the chrome and leather table, keeping
very still as Danny straps his ankles to one pair of legs,
his wrists to the other, so that he is stretched right

across it, down the other side, unable to move except for his head. Frannie, standing in her dragging sense of time, faces an obscenely offered arse, balls hanging heavy below, cock not visible from her view-point, but she can't help looking at the scene from other angles; in one mirror his erection is reflected standing parallel to the underside of the table-top, and the other, in front of him, reflecting a chin resting on chamois, reveals that his teeth are bared in an expression which has no resemblance to a grin and his eyes catch the light and flicker red behind the holes in the black leather mask.

Without warning or preamble, perhaps sensing that he must shock a response into her, Danny leaves the trussed Prinsen, drops to his knees in front of her and begins licking between her legs, an action which, despite her presently frigid disposition, causes her to rest her hands on his shoulders and her legs to sag. She follows this piece of action in the mirrors, her eyes unavoidably drawn to them, and the heat between her legs softens the harshness of the tableau as Danny's finger once again broaches her asshole, and Prinsen's almost hidden eyes watch, his cock throbbing and spasmodically jerking upwards, tapping against the underside of the table. Fellini.

Danny standing, his tongue tracing a damp smear from one nipple to her throat as he does so, his hand sliding up her thigh and finishing where his tongue had left, *gripping* her down there, saying, in its painless intensity, something which is closely allied to this sado-masochistic setting and he kisses her with ferocity then pinches in her cheeks with his free hand, the intensity of his stare freezing her, she stops breathing. He insists, 'Okay, Sweetheart?' She nods weakly, defeated, as he treats her cunt to a bit of extra pressure, almost enough to hurt, then leaves her and, forcing time back into gear with shocking enormity he

133

snatches at one of the perforated paddles on the wall and swings it all the way from there into Prinsen's buttocks. There is a flat sound like an echoless rifle shot which intrudes on Elton John who has moved on to 'Crazy Water', an indrawn gasp from Prinsen, a quivering of the flesh on the back of his thighs and Danny whacks him again and wheels to Frannie, handing her the paddle.

'No harder than that,' he says, bluntly. 'Just enough to sweetly sting,' and, leaving her staring down at the paddle which has suddenly assumed an insidious life of its own, it trembles in her hand, he moves to Prinsen's face where he stands, his cock semi-erect, staring at her across the rubber-clad back and he encourages her, an edge of threat, 'Come on darling, get on with it. He's waiting.' And Frannie, another Frannie, she can see her behind Danny's head, lifts an unwilling hand and swings a wooden paddle into fleshy buttocks already turning pink. Slap! and Danny snarls. *Harder*! and she does. *Whack*! and Danny breathes, 'Yes, like that. Like that', and that other Frannie who belongs not in such a scene begins to warm to her task (it's only a game, after all, no-one gets hurt) as the real Frannie, appalled, deliciously appalled, watches her hand rising and falling on buttocks which are beginning to glow and sees Danny introducing his now rock-hard member into the Dutchman's mouth and each time Frannie connects he thrusts into the lips.

But the little scene was not destined to come to an end in quite that combination. It finished with Danny squatting under the table, Frannie still paddling while Prinsen ejaculated into his mouth. Then Danny took that other Frannie, that wallowing, lost and sordid Frannie, bent her over the bed and quickly fucked her in the arse, a few long, powerful strokes and then he shouted and she felt his sperm flooding into her.

134

Long moments of lying very still, still coupled like that, Frannie has not come, she is keyed right up to it but she's with two spent men; then Prinsen mumbles something and Danny rolls off her, pushes himself to his feet – it takes an effort – and goes to Prinsen and releases him. The Dutchman straightens with a long-drawn-out sigh, moves to the bed and perches himself near Frannie's face where he murmurs, 'My dear Frannie. I must thank you, you have helped in bringing me to a most marvellous moment of ecstacy.' His hand strays to her behind, caresses it, two fingers intrude between her legs, discovering her wetness. 'But we have been too selfish, it is your turn. You must learn what it is to have such an orgasm.'

That other Frannie allows herself to be pulled to her feet, making no resistance as she is led to the wall and is made to face it. Danny straps her hands to a big ring high above her head so that she is stretched taut; without the shoes she would be standing on tip-toes. But then, something new, totally unexpected, she does not like it but it happens before she has time to protest. A rubber ball, attached to a rubber strap, forced into her mouth, the strap buckled behind her head. She noises her dislike – 'Mmm, Mmmm, *Mmmmmm*,' and Prinsen whispers, mouth close to her ear, which he nibbles, 'To bite on. An added pleasure, you'll see.'

She twists her head to look over her shoulder, sees how she is, how she looks trussed like that, in a mirror. The inconceivability of ever having got herself into such a situation with these two perverts suddenly hits her, a massive shock wave rocks her psyche and, frighteningly, she becomes Frannie once more, the need between her legs dissolves away as she watches Danny select a particularly thin and whippy cane, cut the air with it, *Swish*! and hand it to Prinsen.

# 9
# Moveable Feasts

She remembered the ring. A flood-tide of fear had inundated all rational thought but now the feared was reality.

Her hands were strapped together above her head at the wrists, leaving the fingers free. With her thumb and index finger, Frannie took hold of the emerald in the ring on the other hand and turned it a half-revolution clockwise.

Gregory was dozing when the bleeper went off in the top pocket of his jacket. Apart from the practice run in England he had never heard it and, at first, it invaded his dreams as a football referee signalling the end of a match. But in moments his eyes flickered open and, instantly awake, he flung himself out of the Mercedes and sprinted to the door of the house.

Upstairs, as Elton John got into the strident 'One Horse Town', the Dutchman lifted the cane once more.

Only Frannie, whose ears were straining for sounds of Gregory, heard the thump as her bodyguard came in through the front door, the quickest way he knew how, taking a running, flying, two-footed kick at it, all his powerful weight behind his size twelve boots which smashed into the wood by the door catch.

No match for the massive Gregory, the ancient door burst open. He caught his falling self on his hands, executed a back roll and was on his feet all in one smooth motion. Hearing the loud music above, he charged up the stairs which creaked and groaned under him, located the room and, not bothering with the handle, smashed in the door with his shoulder.

The scene which confronted Gregory stopped him for precisely two seconds whilst he assessed it. Prinsen's cane was on its downswing and Gregory saw the full stroke as the Dutchman's hooded head jerked towards him.

An enraged bellow from Gregory. Pushing at Prinsen he smashed a ringed, meaty fist into his mask in the region of the temple and the Dutchman staggered sideways into his friend and dropped to the floor without making a sound. Danny, making the mistake of his life, tried to protect himself with the cane, taking a swing at Gregory who plucked it from his hands as if catching a straw in the wind and, still voicing his rage with roars, mightily furious, began raining blows on him with it, on any place he could reach. As the powerful, punishing blows fell on Danny, on his head, his arms, his genitals, he sunk to a protective crouch on the floor, hands over his ears, screaming for Gregory to stop. Gregory smashed him twice more, lashing the cane across the knuckles of each hand then finished his job off with a karate kick which connected with the point of Danny's chin, breaking it and sending him catapulting into the wall where he slumped, unconscious.

He turned to Frannie. She had watched the ferocious moments with awesome fascination; now she was suddenly, unexpectedly, embarrassed by her nakedness, by the blatancy of the position in which Gregory found her. Too enraged for the nicety of embarrassment he unstrapped her hands and freed her of the rubber gag, then, breathing heavily, trying not to look at her – which was all but impossible since her spike-heeled, corsetted image confronted him from three directions – he snatched up the satin sheet from the bed and thrust it roughly at her. Grateful, she wrapped it around her shoulders.

Rage barely subsiding, he stabbed fierce, searching glances around the room then, not looking at her, he growled, 'Just where are your clothes?'

'Downstairs.' She murmured the word, eyes on the floor.

'Downstairs.' His eyes fell on the open wardrobe, comprehended, blazed. 'You *let* them bring you upstairs naked and dress you like that?'

She nodded, feeling small and still embarrassed. This might have been her father speaking to her, not an employee. The shock of this knowledge served to add fuel to his fire of anger. He stared from one fallen man to the other, speaking in a slow snarl which was only decibels lower than a shout. 'You let these, these filthy *bastards* get you into this, this ...'

She managed, 'It was supposed to be a ... a kind of a game. Make-believe.'

'Make-believe? Make-believe?' He was roaring again, a wounded bull. 'I'll give the fuckers make-believe!'

Reaching into his jacket he brought out a flick-knife and clicked the wicked-looking blade open as he went to Prinsen who was supine, legs apart. Gregory crouched.

Frannie gasped. 'What one earth are you doing?'

He turned his mask of fury on her and snarled. 'I'm going to have their balls, that's what I'm doing!' He reached for the Dutchman.

'No! For God's sake, Gregory. *No!*' She wailed the words, in a panic.

'Oh, *yes!*' He slid the cold, bright edge of the knife blade under Prinsen's testicles as Frannie, the idea of the mutilation sending shivers of horror through her despite what she had been about to suffer in the men's hands, rushed at him and shoved with all her might at

138

his huge shoulder, succeeding in knocking him off-balance. He toppled awkwardly into the side of the bed, the knife slicing into Prinsen's testicles as he fell, but not enough to do permanent damage.

There Gregory remained for long moments, frozen, scared to move because of what he might do, his anger seething and churning within him but becoming rational enough to put up a fight against it. His breathing began to calm, his pulse steadied and, as Elton John switched into the romantic 'Chameleon' he got to his feet and vented the rest of his rage on the stereo, silencing the singer with his first powerful blow, then smashing the equipment into irrepairable pieces.

He stared at his damage for long seconds, glanced disgustedly around the room, then said, quietly, 'Perhaps you ought to be finding your clothes and getting dressed. It's time we got out of here.' He paused. 'My lady.'

'Yes.' At the door she turned. 'Thank you, Gregory.'

'Just doing my job, Lady Ballington.'

'Yes.' As she left the room Gregory took a last, long-ing look at the genitals of the leather-masked Dutchman; blood had stained the insides of his thighs. He tested the keeness of his blade with his thumb, inhaled deeply and held that breath as he reluctantly snapped the knife shut, put it away and followed his mistress down the stairs.

'... and that's when, thank Heavens, Gregory appeared.'

It was early evening. Frannie, having slept most of the day, had taken a shower and was lying face down on her bed in the Amstel Hotel, a fluffy white bathrobe up around her waist as Matilda applied ointment to the welts on her behind. The cuts themselves had healed quickly; two fine scab lines had formed, but the flesh around them was blue and puffy.

'I knew something pretty serious must have happened last night. But Gregory's not telling. He's been in a foul mood all afternoon, I could hardly get a word out of him.'

'I'm not surprised. I've never seen a man so angry. I shocked him quite deeply. I'm sure. Strange, in a way, with his background. And after all, he's employed to protect me, to get me out bad situations. He knew the score from the beginning. Knows it's sex.'

Matilda annointed Frannie's buttocks lovingly, finding the action, and the imagining of the scene which produced the welts, mildly erotic. 'I think Gregory's put you on a pedestal. God knows why. He seems to have some idea of you as a young innocent being seduced into sexual adventure by a wicked old ogre of a husband.'

'It's about time he accepted the truth. He's not entirely stupid.' She shuddered. 'You know that was really turning horrifically nasty last night. Thinking about what must have been going on in those men's heads scares me even now. I was pretty foolish to let myself get that involved.'

Matilda covered the welts with two strips of lint which she secured with plasters. 'There you are.' She feasted her eyes a moment longer on her favourite behind, then pulled down the bathrobe. 'Perhaps,' she said. 'But you, ah, you wouldn't have summoned Gregory had it been what they had made out it was going to be – a nice light spanking.'

Frannie darted a quick look at her. 'Trust you to make a point. I suppose I wouldn't have done, no. But I knew I was in trouble the moment that horrible rubber gag was shoved into my mouth. I could have – should have – used my ring right then. But I didn't. I think I got into a sort of a panic.' She paused. 'I must say, Gregory was absolutely magnificent. The way he exploded in there with no warning, they must have

140

thought they were being attacked by some sort of a fiend out of hell.'

'A lot of damage?'

'I'll say. Danny will need hospital treatment for sure. I don't know about the Dutchman. He was out cold with one blow to the side of his head. Addled his brain, shouldn't wonder. We called for an ambulance before we left the house. Still, it could have been worse.' She told Matilda about the incident with the knife.

'My God. He must really care about you to get that mad.'

'Thank God he didn't know what had gone on before. That they were queers as well as psychopathic sadists. You know what he thinks of queers. He'd have castrated them for sure.'

'I rather wish he had. I don't think I'd have stopped him.'

'*Really*, Matilda!' She turned over on her back, then sat up, curling her legs beneath her. 'Ouch.' Wriggling, she grimaced. 'I'll have to get used to it.'

'Mmmm. Matter of fact, I'm the teeniest bit sore in the same place today.'

'I beg your pardon?'

'Willem, my Dutch boy.' She giggled. 'He insisted that plump bottoms like mine are made for spanking.'

'Oh, God. Of course, he's a friend of theirs.'

'Maybe. But it was nothing like your scene. Over his knees in his little flat. With a nice thin leather slipper. I'm sort of glowing a bit today. There's even one tiny little bruise. Coincidence, no? Would you like to see?'

Frannie gave her a look of mock shock. 'No I would not. The very idea!' She smiled and wrinkled her nose. 'Was it good?'

'Good? Not half. It was delicious.' Clasping her hands between her legs she closed her thighs on them, rocking a little on the edge of the bed as she remembered. 'Some stud, that boy. Actually he's just a casual acquaintance of your two. There's nothing queer, or sadistic, about him.'

'He knows when to stop? You didn't have to stop him?'

'Spanking? Absolutely. And he knows a lot of other things remarkable in a boy of his age. He …'

Frannie broke in. 'Never mind, Matilda. I'll use my imagination. I'm delighted you had such a good time.'

Matilda glanced at her watch. 'I'm due back for some more in a little while. That is, if you don't object.'

'No, of course I don't mind. Better make the most of it though.'

Matilda groaned. 'Oh, no. Not again.'

'I'm afraid so. Tomorrow. Well, you don't think I'm going to stay in this city for much longer, do you, after it's gone sour on me? Besides, those bastards might try to track me down, get some sort of a revenge. They inhabit a pretty tough world, you know. And they only have to ask Tony to find out where I am.'

'Point taken. So where are you planning to whisk us off to now?'

'Spain. Marbella, I thought. That's not so far. You remember that sweet, rather eccentric couple who were house-guests at Stratton last year? Lord and Lady Litford?'

'You mean Sophronia? That hilarious lady who drinks like a fish from morning to night? The one who managed to knock over the bust of Victor's grandfather?'

Frannie smiled. 'And broke the ear off. I have a standing invitation to their house at Marbella. I could do with some sunshine on this bum of mine.'

'Isn't it a touch short notice?'

'I shouldn't think so. They apparently have an enormous place. Let's give it a try.'

As Frannie reached for her address book Matilda pulled the edges of her mouth down in a little grimace.

'I'll be spending half my time dodging that Adrian. Randy old buffer was goosing me at every opportunity last year.'

'Keep you on your toes. Here.' She passed Matilda her open book. 'See if you can reach them, there's a dear.'

Lady Litford was at home, in her usual controlled state of insobriety. She would be delighted to receive them. Then Frannie left a message for her pilot and called Lord Ballington.

The first thing her husband, home at Stratton Castle, told her, was that he had received the photos of the porno Frannie in action. He found them intriguing in the extreme. When she talked about her narrow escape the previous evening his response was a promised five hundred pounds bonus for Gregory. But when she questioned him about his sexual doings in the seemy areas of British cities he surprised her by explaining that he had changed his mind, deciding that he was perhaps getting a little mature for that sort of behaviour. He was going to store his sexual energies for Frannie's return to enjoy in the vicarious pleasure of her stories and recordings. He was filling his spare time at home by getting on with the novel which he had been promising himself for some time to 'have a bash at'.

'Victor's writing a novel,' said Frannie, hanging up.

'Good for him.'

'I'm pleased. He's been talking about it for at least a year.'

'I know. It'll be full of sex, I suppose?'

'Why do you suppose *that*?'

'Well, so much of his life has been so devoted to sex. Since he met you, certainly. I can't say about before.'

'You'd better believe before!'

'There you are then. As I understand it, a book is built around what a man knows about.'

'He knows about other things Matilda, for God's sake.'

Matilda did not appear to hear that. 'We'll all be in it, of course. He's probably spreading me naked all over the pages right now!'

Frannie giggled. 'It'll be what is known as a meaty novel, then.'

'Thanks very much.'

'Sorry.' She glanced at the grandfather clock in a corner of the room. 'Didn't you have a date?'

'Absolutely. I must go.'

As Matilda reached the door, Frannie had a wicked moment. 'What is it tonight, spanking or screwing?'

She paused with her hand on the knob, looking over the top of her glasses at a Frannie she could not see. 'It had jolly well better be both!' she said.

# 10
# Falling In Love

For once Gregory was excused the duty of driving. Frannie's party was met at Malaga Airport by the chauffeur-driven Litford Bentley, Lord Litford's pride and joy, twenty years old and in mint condition, and driven in old-fashioned style through the rambling, sprawling, coastal towns of Torremolinos and Fuengirola, a mess of overdeveloped tourism, and finally the one-time fishing village of Marbella itself, a town which had retained much of its charm despite a boom period of growth.

Lord and Lady Litford's residence in the jet-set playground of Marbella was better described as a mansion than a house. Fronting the beach close to Prince Alfonso Hohenlohe's world-famous Marbella Club Hotel, it rose majestically among mature pine trees in three acres of gardens which rolled gently down to the Mediterranean. Only five years old, the house had been designed and built in the massive proportions of a castle. All the walls, interior and exterior, were a minimum of four feet thick, those in the living and dining areas and in the grand hallway towering up into vaulted, hand-carved oak ceilings. A six feet high, eight feet wide, hewn grey stone fireplace with the Litford arms over it dominated the main living area which, in deference to the semi-tropical climate, was floored in a white marble which was host to assorted colourful rugs, enough plush armchairs and sofas to seat a small army, and a card-corner with two green baize tables set amongst an indoor garden of monstrous plants. In the banquet room seventy people could be seated for dinner, and throughout the house more than two hundred could relax in comfort and frequently did since the Litfords, renowned party givers, had built their home with the idea of filling it with people. Yet, despite its vastness, Las Brisas – The Breezes –, as the house was named, managed to be warm and friendly. Its comfortable furniture, its rugs and tapestries, its sculptures and paintings, the genial, eccentric hosts themselves, welcomed you as part of one big, if rather exclusive, international family.

The oval driveway, capable of accommodating up to a hundred cars was host to only three when the Bentley parked. Frannie and Matilda were escorted by a liveried butler through a huge patio with a square ornamental pool, alive with fish, to the entrance hall while Gregory and the chauffeur disappeared in another direction with luggage.

It was shortly after lunch and Lady Litford, tipsily good-humoured, bright eyes dancing in a somewhat puffy, regal face, greeted them in that grand hallway by a backgammon table which had hosted thousands of high-staked games. A cigarette in a holder in one hand, half-full glass in the other, she bent forward slightly to be kissed on either cheek as the randy Lord Litford appeared, arms outstretched, saying stridently, 'I say, how *nice* to see you, Frannie. How *exceptionally* nice,' Whilst his eyes strayed to Matilda's fleshy bosom.

Having endured Litford's splashy kiss on her cheek, Frannie said, 'You remember Matilda, of course? She lives with us at Stratton. She's my travelling companion.'

'Of course, my dear. How are you?' said Lady Litford. 'You must have the orange room. And for you

Frannie, I've had the pink one prepared. Itsh,' – she corrected herself – 'Whoops! *It's* your sort of colour.' She took what appeared to be a very determined slug from her glass. 'And how is dear Victor? Why isn't he with you?'

'He's writing a novel.'

'How splendid,' Lord Litford pronounced. 'Bit foolish of him though, I'd say, letting a gorgeous bit of fluff like you gallivant around the world. Get into all sorts of trouble. What?'

He received an adm nishing glance from his wife. 'Do behave, Adrian. You can't go describing Lady Ballington as a bit of fluff. My Gawd!'

'What? Don't see why not.'

Frannie laughed. 'I don't think I mind.' Then she coughed as she watched the lanky lord's jaundiced eye as it left her and travelled quickly over Matilda's curves.

Later as Matilda unpacked for her in the pink room, which was very pink indeed but with a great charm, Frannie remarked, 'The good Lord Litford seems to have a certain appreciation of your fleshy charms.'

Matilda snorted. 'Wonderful for me.'

'You should try and woo him from Sophronia.'

'That'll be the day anybody convinces him to leave her. He doesn't have a penny of his own, you know.'

'Really? I had no idea.'

'I thought it was common knowledge.' As she carefully hung Frannie's clothes in a wardrobe, Matilda went on, 'They were only married, oh, ten, eleven years ago. He was quite broke. Taking his seat in the House just for the stipend, doing public relations, appearing on company boards because they wanted a title, that sort of thing. Of course they'd known each other for years and had always been fond of each other. She'd outlived one title, wanted another. He craved for a lifestyle to match his breeding. Bingo! The perfect match.'

'It does seem to work rather well, actually. You should have found something like that.'

Matilda smiled wistfully. 'I've told you before, not for lack of trying. But I'm perfectly happy as I am.'

'Small mercies, I suppose.'

Matilda turned from the wardrobe, arms akimbo. 'To change the subject, forgive me for saying, but I think a long rest is the order of the day now that we're here.'

'Oh? From what, may I ask?'

'Men. What else?'

Kicking off her shoes, Frannie perched on the pink bedspread of the pink canopied bed. 'Perhaps you have a point. But sex, new experiences, men, they *are* the whole idea behind this trip. Remember?'

'And are you sure you're still enjoying it?'

'What an odd question. Of course I'm enjoying it!'

'Even after the other night?' Matilda began arranging underclothes in a drawer.

Frannie considered. 'Even after the other night. There were a lot of things about the other night which were amusing, arousing in the strangest of ways. And I learned certain things about myself. I surprised myself. That frightful twist at the end even had its value.'

'How can you say that?'

'Because it did. It taught me a much-needed lesson about my own naïvety. It showed me that there is a sexual line which is dangerous to cross. That something wholly evil in men can show its face under certain circumstances.'

'Only men who are sick to start with.'

Frannie glanced sharply at her. 'I wonder. I hope you're right. I certainly don't intend to find out again, to let anything get that far again. But I'm pleased to have had the experience. I got kicks which I won't forget in a hurry. If ever.'

'Sometimes I find you strange.' Matilda closed the lid of an empty suitcase and shoved it under the bed.

'End of interrogation. By the way, how's your – er – your rear end?'

Frannie raised an eyebrow. 'That's a question, coming from you. How's yours?'

She touched it, grinning. 'Comfortable, thank you. It's got another little bruise.'

'I'll bet.' Frannie studied Matilda. She was in fine humour. The sun streaming through the windows was hot on her and suddenly, as so often happened at unexpected moments, tempting, erotic thoughts stole upon her. Quietly, she said, 'I'm still a bit sore. Why don't you rub a bit more cream in?'

'Mmmm,' said Matilda, catching Frannie's mood. 'What a lovely idea. Take your drawers off then.'

A stirring in Frannie's guts. She was wearing hand-cut slacks by the English designer Blue: no stockings underneath, just a simple pair of white silk panties. Pants and slacks came off together and she lay face down on the bed. Her behind was still adorned with the two stripes of lint from the previous evening.

'Hold your breath,' said Matilda. She took hold of one strip at the top and ripped it away from Frannie's flesh with a quick jerk, the three plasters tearing clear of her buttock sounding like a zipper. Frannie gasped, her sudden intake of breath hardly over before the second piece of lint was ripped clear in the same way and she gasped again.

'Thanks very much!' She exclaimed.

Matilda leant close to her ear, said softly, 'You mean you didn't *enjoy* it?'

'Idiot.'

Matilda examined the damaged area. 'Much better,' she proclaimed. 'The swelling's gone down and the bruises are a shade lighter. A bit more of the soothing ointment rubbed well in, I think. No need for another dressing.'

Wriggling to get more comfortable, Frannie took a

pillow from under the coverlet, wrapped her arms around it and buried her cheek in it, anticipating the familiar touch of Matilda's fingers, the heat of the sun on her naked behind adding to her growing feeling of sensuality. At Matilda's first, caressing touch, she tensed and as the cream was gently rubbed into her skin, her buttocks began to tighten and slacken as she shoved her crotch with increasing need into the softness of the bed. To Matilda the message was clear. The sacred wounds annointed, she turned her expert attentions to the more urgent necessity, slipping her index and second fingers deep inside Frannie's already wet hole.

Frannie moaned. Then she murmured, as Matilda worked her fingers slowly up and down her. 'Yes, darling, yes. That. Then let me look at your little bruises.'

For five, sun-drenched days Frannie did very little. Early June in Marbella has a tendency to be idyllic and this year was no exception. The town was relatively quiet, resting up for the mad months to come, and she got in some leisurely shopping in establishments which, only a few years previously before the British invasion, would never have considered putting down roots in the old fishing town, expensive shops bearing names like Cartier and Giorgio and Ted Lapidus.

When not shopping, she relaxed by the pool amongst the pine trees or went naked on the almost deserted stretch of beach which the grounds fronted, the sun on her bare rear end doing a wonderful job of obliterating the evidence of her creepy night in Amsterdam.

The late afternoons brought games players to the house; there were lively chouettes at backgammon and games of bridge or gin rummy. Frannie joined in each afternoon's backgammon and lost cheerfully, no match for the high standard of most of the players who included on two occasions world champion Paul Magriel. Evenings were spent at lengthy, entertaining dinner parties, the guests usually distinguished in one way or another even if only for their money. These would be followed by visits to Regine's, or Menchu's, or to the oldest discotheque in Marbella, Pepe Moreno, founded over a quarter of a century ago.

There were no men. That is to say, Frannie found herself in a mood to refuse invitations from men whom she would normally find attractive enough. It seemed that, perhaps after all, that Holland night had had a subtle effect on her, the 'no's', when she said them, sounded a bit illogical to herself, considering her overall mission.

But on the evening of the fifth day she found herself plunged into a situation totally unexpected and unprepared for. It was Sophronia Litford's fifty-eighth birthday, and there was a huge, informal party, an open-house affair in which anyone who was in any way known socially to the Litfords was welcome without the need for invitation. People began to arrive shortly after nine in the evening and the house was filling by ten, guests attacking a massive buffet table spread with everything from partridge through lobster to Iranian caviar. The usual Marbella celebrity faces showed up: Queen Fabiola's brother Jaime de Mora Y Aragon, Philip Junot, Gunilla von Bismark, assorted titles both real and false, movie stars Sean Connery, Linda Christian, Omar Sharif.

Frannie and Matilda – Frannie in a fine silver lamé evening gown from Adele Simpson which clung to her supple body as graciously as the skin of a fish – were sitting close to the stone fireplace, dinner plates balanced on their knees. It was a good vantage point with a view through an archway into the great hall where new arrivals made their entrance. Frannie was making sport with Matilda about the behaviour of Lord Litford who had been pursuing her at every opportunity.

'I really can't see why you don't let him have you,' she said, through a mouthful of lobster. 'You never know you might enjoy it.'

'Come off it, Frannie. How can you say such a thing? He's about thirty-five years older than me, to start with.' Matilda sipped white wine. She was in black velvet, with one simple string of cultured pearls, both items legacies from her mother.

'Experience counts. He's possibly the most powerful of lovers.'

'*Do* cut it out. The mind boggles. My God, those ears. The way he slobbers. That nose!'

'It's supposed to relate to the size of his thing. Did you know that?' Frannie's words tailed off as her fork stopped halfway between plate and mouth, hovering there and she stared through the archway. 'Who's *that*? I know that face.'

It was a man, very tall and straight, with especially broad shoulders and a tight body which tapered to narrow hips. He was dressed in a plain white tailored cotton shirt, a wisp of colour at his throat, well-cut jeans and very shiny, well-worn black boots. He looked to be about forty and had dark brown hair, cut quite short. He was wearing big, Porsche shaded glasses. As he shook Lord Litford's hand he seemed completely at ease in his casual attire which was in direct contrast with his host's conservatively cut cream linen suit and old school tie.

Frannie found herself unable to take her eyes off the man. 'Who *is* he?' she breathed. 'What a stunning looking example of the male species!'

'You know damn well I can't see past the end of my nose. Hang on.' Fumbling in her evening bag Matilda produced her bi-focals, jammed them on her nose and squinted into the hall. 'Oh, my gosh,' she said. 'Of course you know who it is. It's David Donnelly.' She stared. 'My gosh,' she said again.

David Donnelly was the current big American heartthrob movie hero, his extraordinary fame enough to eclipse that of all the other celebrities at the party. His latest film, *The Suicide Man*, had carried off six Oscars and he had the Oscar for the best actor of 1986.

'Is it, indeed? Well, well.' Frannie did not normally turn the slightest hair over celebrities but in this instance she was more than impressed. She found the physical presence of the flesh and blood David Donnelly, even at that distance, as strong as that of his powerful screen self.

Litford carried him off somewhere and for a while he was lost in the throng. Then Lord Litford, even taller than Donnelly, hanging onto his arm with one hand, the star clearly his catch of the evening, brought him to them. As the two materialised in front of them Matilda scrabbled her glasses back in her bag and Frannie ran a self-conscious hand through her hair.

Litford's ruddy face was beaming with pleasure as he made the introductions. Matilda was so flustered that she stood up.

'How do you do,' said Frannie, cooly, offering her hand, finding it taken with a smooth pressure which sent an unaccountable tingle up her arm. Which was nothing compared with the sensation which hit her next as he removed his glasses and said in his familiar, resonant, slightly southern American voice, 'Hi. Adrian's been telling me about you. He doesn't lie. Evidently he understates.'

The potency of his charisma stirred Frannie's psyche as she found herself staring into the richest, deepest pair of chestnut eyes she had ever seen, incapable of looking away, giddy almost, holding her breath but her composure only just as she all but stammered,

'That's very kind of you.'

The hands remained clasped, the eyes locked, longer than protocol called for, Frannie feeling an inexplicably deep, silent communication between them, until Lord Litford cleared his throat with exaggerated loudness, breaking their physical contact, but not the spell which had been woven on Frannie, and carted the star off to continue his rounds.

'Oh my golly,' said Matilda, sitting down, poking her face close to Frannie's. 'Just look at you!'

Frannie was perfectly still except for her eyes which followed the two men's backs, her mouth open, clearly stunned. She said, almost inaudibly, her lips barely moving, 'Something unbelievable has just happened to me.' She turned her wide eyes to Matilda. 'Only I don't quite know what it is.'

For the next hour she did nothing but try to catch sight of Donnelly as the party blurred around her. Twice, when she did, he smiled briefly at her and she felt her heart thumping as she did lip-service to smiles in return. Making the effort of socialising with Matilda, moving from group to group, she was quite unaware of what was said to her, or what she said in return. She sought only the opportunity to get together with David Donnelly.

It happened when she and Matilda strolled out down to the swimming pool for a breath of fresh air. There was only a handful of people outside yet Frannie was unaware of any approach; he was just suddenly there, at her side.

He said, 'What a terrific night. Can't think why most everybody's inside.'

'Gosh. Oh. Hello!' fumbled Matilda.

Frannie went weak in the knees, but when she spoke she managed to sound contained. 'Lovely, isn't it? Warm enough for a swim.'

'I dare you.'

'Please don't. Dares tempt me and I'm really not in that sort of a mood.' So far she had been avoiding his eyes; now they caught her. An incredible feeling threatened to overwhelm her; they were brown pools, she was tumbling right in.

'You enjoy temptation?'

'Only for its own sake. Not always what it might lead me into.' She was getting into a strange conversation which had nothing to do with what she felt. Impulsively, she said, 'May I call you David?' Their eyes were still locked.

'It's my name.'

There was something very much like an electric force generating between them, overpowering the superficiality of the words and Matilda, her presence totally excluded by this tension, said, 'Er, I, I think I'll just get myself another drink,' and walked away with a full glass.

'I'm Frannie. But you know that. That is, everybody calls me Frannie.' She felt the need to keep talking. 'Actually it's Frances.'

'Pretty.' There was a long pause, pregnant with those vibrations. 'Nowhere near as pretty as its owner, though.'

'Oh.' She tore her eyes away from his; it took the same effort as ripping a sheet, and looked at the perfectly still water of the pool. 'Thank you.' Her voice had gone very small. She was engulfed, yet something deep inside her head told her she was not entirely happy at what was happening to her.

He touched her elbow and the simple contact caused her an inner shudder. 'May I walk you around the garden?'

'Please.'

They strolled and talked nothings for half an hour, Frannie's senses continuing to overwhelm anything which was spoken, her mind refusing to be in two

155

places at once, except that an infinitely tiny warning light was glowing there. Then they came back to the pool, where there was now nobody. Music and laughter drifted out from the house; overhead, a fine sliver of moon hung among the sharpest of stars. They stopped there and he turned her to face him. He said, quietly, 'May I be very presumptuous?'

'Oh.' She knew with an absolute certainty what was going to happen next. 'If you want.' A pine needle dropped into the pool, creating a disturbance disproportionate to its size.

'I need to kiss you.'

She looked up at him. Weak. 'You need …?'

'I need.' Enfolding her in his arms he kissed her with a sublime tenderness, she so losing herself in him as he did, his eyes and lips were swallowing her psyche, that she got the impression that, if he let her go, what was left of her would collapse into a heap at his feet.

It was a first kiss which lasted until the water of the pool was quite still again and, when it was over, he held her at arms' length, studying her as if she were some long-lost art treasure. 'You're really quite exceptionally wonderful,' he said, quietly. Then he said, 'Am I being horribly forward?'

'You're not taking advantage of the who-you-are thing?'

'No. I'm putting into a practice an urge which has been with me since that first moment we met. The way it stretched time has been unbearable.'

'You have an eloquent way of making love.'

'Am I making love?'

'I believe you are, yes.'

He grinned a lop-sided grin which momentarily turned him into a college kid. 'Not my usual approach.'

'I don't know if I believe that.'

'You must. I don't believe I can feel what I'm feeling, without you feeling it the same way.'

Frannie sighed and looked away from him. That red light in her mind was a tiny fraction brighter. Her inner self was taking a severe beating and, recognizing that, she also recognized that she was being swamped with emotions she did not want, which were not on her agenda because they would lead her into a dangerous situation from which not even Gregory could extricate her.

'I feel what you're feeling, yes.' Making a supreme effort she shrugged out of his hands. 'So I think I'd better go back inside.' And she turned and began to walk away from him, forcing her legs to do what her mind was trying to tell them to while her heart screamed out against it.

He let her go. That is, he let her take seven, tortuous steps. Then he called after her, question in his voice. 'Francisca?'

She faltered, his voice, the unexpected use of the Spanish equivalent of her name, contriving to stop her. But she took another step, and another, the partying house ahead offering her some sort of crazy sanctuary from emotions she did not want to have to cope with. Then he was with her, grasping her elbows, spinning her around. She gasped. He took her face by the chin and kissed her as sweetly as tenderly, as lovingly as the first time. But this time in that kiss there was also implicit a sexual hunger.

The kiss, the pounding of her heart, the churning of her stomach, combined to make her breathless. As their lips parted she inhaled deeply, held it, and finally let it out as a sigh. 'You shouldn't be … be doing this to me, David. You have no right.'

'Then you have no right to do it to me.'

She listened to the words which spilled next from her mouth with something close to incredulity. 'I don't want to be in love.'

'That's what it is, isn't it? The legendary love at first

sight.' He pulled her to him and kissed her again, less tender, a rising passion. Then he said, those big chestnut eyes conveying as much as his words, 'What could be more wonderful?'

'Yes. I mean, no ... no, I ...' She was lost.

'What?'

'It can't be happening. It mustn't. It just can't be. I'm married, I love my husband. I don't *want* this. I ...'

He stopped her words with another kiss. Then he said. 'So you're married. I hardly expected otherwise. You love your husband, who am I to argue? Then what is this?' He searched her face.

'This is craziness, that's what it is.'

'A fine and beautiful craziness, I'd say.'

'Oh, God. Where the hell did you come from?'

'A little town called Hugoton in Kansas, as a matter of fact.'

'Good for Hugoton.' She began to get angry with herself. That rational part of her mind which had got her feet taking her back into the house still fought for control. Incredibly, it now tried another tactic, attempted to dirty this experience, to turn it into just another adventure. 'Okay, Mr David Donnelly from Hugoton, Kansas,' she found herself saying, 'Let's fuck!'

His mouth dropped open. '*What?*'

'I'm sure you understand good, old-fashioned English. That's what we really want, isn't it? That's what this is all about.' She took his hand, started leading him down the sloping lawn. 'So let's do it. Down in the pine trees. A zipper fuck I believe that's known as.'

After a few paces he stopped her. 'What are you doing? What are you trying to do?'

'Get us laid.' She tugged at him. 'Come on, I want to fuck.' The extraordinary thing was that at that moment she did not.

David Donnelly jerked her arm, hurting her. He raised his voice. 'Stop that, you hear? You just stop it. I don't want to hear this. Shut up with that talk.'

She was done. She looked for similar words but they refused to come. Trembling with her complication of emotions, she whispered, 'Sorry,' and leant into him. He wrapped his hefty arms around her. Tears were beginning to well in her eyes and she wiped them away with a self-deprecating little laugh. 'Hasn't happened to me since my favourite spaniel died,' she said.

'You're the strangest girl.'

'Stranger than you know.' She lifted her face. 'Kiss me?'

He did, and this time her mind kept out of the way. Then he murmured, 'Having got whatever all that was about over and done with, may I now say it?'

'Yes.'

'I love you.'

'I know,' she said. 'Oh, *shit*!'

She sneaked him up to her pink bedroom where he stripped her naked with a controlled tenderness, leaving no bits of female fripperie on her flesh to stimulate the erotic and she, habitual diver on the zipper, started to undress him at his neck, the colourful bit of scarf, then his shirt, a kiss on revealed flesh after each button.

Then she had him sit on the bed while she heaved off his boots finding no socks beneath. Lastly he stood while she, in a crouch, unbelted and unzipped him, taking his trousers and pants down together so that he could step out of them, staying in that crouch, mesmerised by the sight of the cock of her new lover-to-be standing swollen in front of her eyes. Locked in those moments with her, he was still and quiet, but it was a tranquillity with undercurrents of fine tension. As he rested his hands on her shoulders, watching, she reached a hand for him and almost reverently ran fingers and thumb from the base of his male shaft to its head, once only, but an exploration of rapt wonderment as if she had never seen one before. Briefly, tenderly, she cupped his balls, feeling their weight as she took his cock once into the warmth of her mouth then brought her head back and off it, tongue trailing saliva on its underside. She looked up into his eyes, his cock brushing her cheek.

'I'm ready to be loved,' she said.

It was making love, but it was fucking, of course, it was fucking, but it was fucking with that extra, powerful dimension to it, which moved the earth for Hemingway, which Mailer might describe as being engaged in a vision with each other. When he first impaled her, Frannie on her back on the pink bedspread, it was so much more for her than the familiar, simple act of a penis sliding into her that it brought an agonised sob to her lips. This entire man, this superstar stranger whom she had suddenly known for more than all of her life, took a possession of her which was spiritual in its completeness. His cock, fucking her with love, her cunt, responding with love, became the embodiments of their souls. The All of their beings slid into a One.

Lady Ballington was unquestionably in love.

# 11
# Islands In The Sun

Being in love, Frannie found, was for her rather like living inside a bubble. The shape of the world around you distorted, your bubble could float you right over it, you were living in a different dimension.

In the ensuing two days Frannie and David made love at every opportunity, managing to conceal the fact from Lord and Lady Litford. Frannie did not want to upset these old family friends of her husband by flaunting her lover in front of them. He had a rented bungalow at the Marbella Club Hotel, a short walk along the beach from Las Brisas, which was where Frannie spent a great deal of her time. But she found it difficult to get out of the regular afternoon backgammon game. David played too and the occasional opportunity for a surreptitious touch of fingers, a stolen meaningful glance, was taken with adolescent excitement. Whilst they played they used their bubbles for protection (Frannie assumed David had one too) hiding their love for each other inside, with themselves, except during those secret, galvanising little moments.

She began to know the man behind the image. Their ids had of course recognized a certain very special something about each other from the beginning and now she found that that primitive inner self seldom makes mistakes. She realized that he was possessed of a fine nobility of spirit. Great actor that he was, he was no lover of the cinema world, holding the opinion that it was akin to a hallucinogenic drug, distorting the vision of all who worked in it. Acting itself he was dedicated to, when he was doing it, infinitely preferring the stage to the screen because of its intimate contact with the audience and its greater possibility, in general, of projecting a whole real character. When not working he divorced himself, as far as he was able, from the world of entertainment. He was a *bon viveur* with a variety of interests which included good literature, fine art, excellent wines, gourmet food when he could find it, the very best Havana cigars in which he indulged only rarely, and music from Beethoven to Dylan. He would have got entirely out of the cinema world but for a solid streak of pragmatism which constantly reminded him that he needed that sort of money to support his life-style. Besides, his emotional past was fairly chaotic; at the comparatively young age of forty-three there were two ex-wives and three children in the background, all of whom he supported royally.

She came to adore the way in which he treated other people. No one was beneath him, too menial for a smile, a please or a thank you; but he related to such people not in the normal condescending manner of the rich but rather as an equal.

The morning after their explosive meeting they had coffee together on the terrace of the Bar Sport in the middle of old Marbella across from the municipal gardens. Two wretched-looking gypsy children with sun-blackened, dirty faces and ragged, filthy clothes, children of professional beggars who were considered by most the scourge of the town, approached their table. One of them put a cheap, gaudy trinket in front of Frannie on the table and said something to David who produced a hundred peseta coin and gave it to her. Looking at it in dismay she held out her hand for more and, smiling, David shook his head, spoke to her

162

and handed the trinket back, both the dirty faces beamed radiance and they skipped away.

'What was all that about?' asked Frannie.

'Oh, nothing. They wanted two hundred pesetas for that piece of junk and when I gave them one they thought that was all they were getting. They didn't expect the thing back.'

'Why did you do that?' she said. 'It was a lovely thing to do.'

'Well,' he drawled, 'Because they're my kids, I guess.'

'They're *your* kids?'

'In a manner of speaking. I'm really only a gypsy at heart.'

Of course, she had not understood that remark then, but she would come to some little comprehension of it as time went by.

On the evening of day two they stole an hour together between backgammon and dinner, to which he was invited. They made love and as they lay naked on the bed afterwards, David said, 'Have you ever been to the Canary Islands?'

'No. But they sound very exotic.' She nuzzled his hairy chest.

'It's a deceiving name. They're not the way people imagine, all lush and tropical, that sort of thing. They're volcanic, often very barren. But they are possessed of a timeless magic.'

Lifting her head, she looked at him. 'Explain.'

'It's difficult. I'm neither poet nor painter enough to do that.' He was an accomplished amateur in both. 'I'd have to show you.'

'Sounds good.'

'I've got a house on one of the islands, as a matter of fact. On Lanzarote.'

'Have you? I've heard of it, of course.'

'I think the essence of the magic is to be found there.

It reaches the other islands but there are certain places there where it's at its most evocative.' He stroked her hair. 'You fancy it?'

'I can't wait.' She paused. 'But I have to warn you that I habitually travel with Matilda and my chauffeur.'

'We can't go in search of magic with a fucking entourage!'

'Oh.' She fluffed the hairs on his chest. 'Well, I'm afraid it's going to be the teeniest bit tricky. I can hardly go off with you and leave them at the Litfords, can I?'

He pulled a face. 'Point taken, I guess.'

'Good. Besides, I promised my husband I wouldn't go any place without them.'

He stopped her lips with his finger. 'No talk of husbands, okay?'

She smiled. 'Okay.'

'You were already planning on going other places then, not home?'

'Yes. And I've already been places.'

'So, where are you booked into next?'

'Nowhere. I go where the whim takes me.'

'That's a fairly odd way of doing things. And extravagant.'

'I suppose it is.' She wondered what his reaction would be if he were to discover the purpose behind her travels, experiencing a little stab of fear at the idea of him finding out.

He was silent for a minute or so, while she lay with an ear against his chest, listening to his heart-beat, supremely comfortable in her bubble. Then he said, 'Look, I guess we can take your people along. But I'd rather they didn't stay at the house with us. I want that to be just us and the old couple who look after me down there. I'll check them into a decent hotel on the island. We can all take the same plane if you like, but you and I will go first class.'

Frannie smiled. 'All right. Of course we'll take the same plane. And we'll all go first class because we'll take my jet!' She thoroughly enjoyed this little revelation.

'Did I hear that right? Did you happen to say your jet?'

She kissed his chest. 'I happened. I have a rather comfortable little Lear, David.'

His mud-pool eyes were wide. 'You seem to be inordinately wealthy.'

'What is known in England as stinking bloody rich, actually.' She giggled, then reached a hand down over his tight belly. 'Is there time before dinner?'

Lanzarote, from the air, stretched out no welcoming arms. The coastline to the south of Arrecife Airport presented a chain of featureless, ribbon tourist development, kilometre after kilometre of it all built over the previous few years on what had been an empty coastal plain with its only saving grace a seemingly endless golden beach. The airport sat in the same characterless plain which extended in a gentle climb to low volcanic mountains the colour of rusty iron.

But then there was the immediate surprise of the airport itself. Frannie had never seen a terminal building remotely like it. It was, of course, quite small. The walls and ceilings were patterned blue fabric criss-crossed with bamboo, the different areas were separated by delicate matt blue trellisses, the bench seats were both colourful and comfortable; music filled the air. The feeling was more that of being in a rather agreeable discotheque than in an airport building.

Matilda and Gregory with the pilot and stewardess all piled into one taxi and set off for their hotel in Arrecife itself while Frannie and David took off in another in the opposite direction, towards the volcanic mountains.

For a while the landscape was as bleak and

depressing as suggested from the air, but soon they were heading through a wide mountain pass and into a low plain of symmetrical and unique beauty. The land before them, rising gradually for three or four miles before them into the foothills of a mountain which, in the distance, appeared quite black, was a sea of black volcanic ash, the grains the size of pieces of rice, and these had been scooped into thousands of circular craters, about six feet in diameter. The craters each had a semi-circular wall of black volcanic rock, all of them on the same side and they were filled with healthy-looking, lightish green plants. Each one was precisely equidistant from its neighbours, creating perfectly geometric, green and black landscape.

David squeezed Frannie's thigh. 'Here it begins,' he said. 'The magic.'

The taxi windows were wide open, it was a balmy day and, indeed, Frannie could sense something special in the sweet-smelling air. 'What are they growing here?' she asked.

'It's a vineyard, a grape plantation, Canary style. The grapes produce a distinct, superb wine. Volcanic ash is extremely fertile, but it's also very light, a strong wind moves it almost as easily as it shifts sand. Hence the scoops and the walls against the prevailing wind.'

They drove past a number of women working in the ash. They had on big straw hats, tied with ribbons under their chins, and wore brightly-coloured, silk-like dresses. 'They actually work like that? In those lovely clothes?' Frannie commented.

'There's nothing to get them dirty or to tear the dresses. You take a handful of that stuff and rub it into your palms, nothing happens. It's clean and soft.' He paused, squeezing her thigh again, higher up. 'Like you.'

She closed her hand over his, raising an eyebrow. 'You rub your palms over me, and something happens

166

all right!' she said.

He grinned. 'You can say that again.' Then he pointed. 'Look, up there. That's where my house is.'

They were approaching the foothills to the old volcano ahead, most of the grape plantation behind them. What had appeared in the distance as a black mountain was mostly just that; two thirds of the side of the mountain ahead of them was a solidified, ebony lava flow, bordered by a wedge-shaped area, from bottom to top, where the lava had not reached and which was covered in a scrubby vegetation. A road cut up into the flow and, perched on it, there were several houses, startlingly white in contrast, sunlight bouncing off them as brightly as off a field of snow. As they approached, Frannie saw that the borders of each house's territory were defined by big volcanic rocks, their colours sliding from the palest of greys through to the darkest of browns, to black again, strategically planted with cacti, some as tall as a man, many in bloom.

Frannie was enthralled, 'It's so extraordinary,' she said.

'It's another world,' said David. 'And here we are.'

The taxi came to a stop at rustic wooden gates. Beyond them was a big arch topped by a bell, fronting what appeared to be a very small house indeed. 'This is it?' Frannie exclaimed.

'Yup. But it's a lot bigger than it looks.'

At the arch David tugged a rope. An old bell clanged hollowly. 'Cracked,' he said.

They were greeted by a couple who seemed to be at least as ancient as the island itself, whose walnut faces, as lined and wrinkled as old leather boots, broke into delighted, toothless smiles as they welcomed them.

What appeared to be about half the house was a roomy entrance hall with a sloping, beamed ceiling, stained-glass windows and walls which were not quite

167

straight. A door led into a simple, rustic-style kitchen and open-planned dining area. Through another door of this, ajar, Frannie could see a black and white television screen flickering. David nodded towards it. 'That's the old people's quarters.'

Which seemed to be it. The area taken as a whole was about right from what it appeared from the outside. Mystified, a touch worried, Frannie said, 'Where do we sleep? In the hall or the kitchen?'

He laughed. 'There's more to this than meets the eye. Let's see the rest of the house.' In one corner of the kitchen was a large, intricately carved, antique wooden screen. Behind it, a spiral staircase, and David, clearly enjoying his big surprise, led the way down.

It took them into one of the most incredible-looking rooms Frannie had ever seen. She stopped three steps from the bottom of the spiral staircase, staring around in confused amazement. She was in a section of a massive white sphere, the walls as smooth as glass. A marble floor dissected this sphere half way between its middle and its base. It was like a huge ping-pong ball with the bottom cut off; a number of circular, coffee table-sized windows brought light into it down shafts. The walls of the sphere were adorned with murals reminiscent of Paul Klee; the furniture, in contrast to the rustic kitchen above them, was clean cut and modern, but wood and glass, no plastic. A sunken seating area, eight feet square had three of its sides padded as sofa backs, touching a white carpeted floor which was strewn with cushions; on the fourth side was a TV, video, stereo and a bar. The room was at least forty feet in diameter which meant that it extended well outside the limit of the walls of the little house above it.

David was watching Frannie with an amused smile. 'Well,' he said, 'What do you think?'

'I don't know quite what I'm thinking,' she murmured. 'What is it exactly? It's not a cave, though it seems like one.'

'In its unpainted state it's a black bubble which was formed by gases trapped in the lava as it solidified. It's great. The temperature never varies, it needs no heat, no cooling.' He paused. 'Come on down from there, I'll show you the rest.'

A short passage led to a second bubble, bigger even than the first, but this one had been divided by walls and a passage into four bedrooms with en-suite baths. Three were regular-sized, except for the great height of the curving outer walls, and the fourth, a door in the end of the passage leading into it, was enormous, one third of the sphere.

Frannie's eyes were drawn to the bed, huge and inviting, spread with a colourful patchwork quilt. David said, 'Lay down on it, on your back. It has a very special view.'

She did. Above her, a six feet diameter shaft, windows at either end, had been let into the ceiling. She saw a sky which was blue except for a few whisps of cloud. Thirty thousand feet above her a jet was tracing a vapour trail.

'At night it's sensational,' said David.

'I'll just bet.'

He joined her on the bed, on his side, leaning on an elbow. 'I love you as much as all of those nights,' he said.

She turned her head to him. 'That's a funny thing to say.'

'It's a gypsy thing to say.'

'You and your gypsy.'

'He's just about as real, or as unreal, as anything.'

'Bubbles in bubbles.'

'Huh?'

'You take me, inside my bubble and you in yours,

and you put those bubbles in another one. Does that mean something? Is it real or unreal?'

'You're talking a sort of pretty nonsense.' He paused. 'This means something.' He began to undo the buttons of her blouse. She smiled. Both her hands, fingers intertwined, were behind the back of her head, her elbows pointing upwards, and she stayed like that, closing her eyes, quite still, exploring her emotions as he undressed her.

Lovers' hands gentling cool bare skin beneath the open blouse, sliding under the bottom edge of her skimpy bra, pushing it up, freeing her breasts to his eyes, his touch, his lips, his tongue as her nipples harden and her forearms close against her ears. The tongue licking its way down her belly, finding her navel, its tip dwelling in that little hole. Her neck arches tighter back into her hands and she holds her breath, letting it out slowly as she feels fingers on the zipper at the side of her fine leather skirt and she raises her bottom just enough so that he can slide it down and off her. Shoes, panties, suspender belt, stockings, are removed with a sweet, painful slowness, and the familiar, welcome need grows steadily within her; but she contrives to keep quite still as hands part her thighs, teeth nibble on her little bud of a clitoris, and then she moves, her groin tenses and pushes into his face as his tongue finds its way inside her. Little moans of pleasure escape her lips, her hands unclasp and find the back of her lover's head, her eyes come half open and she stares at the sky as her legs are parted at the knees, and in that attitude he leaves her.

There are moments when she is untouched, she cannot see him but she senses him as he removes his trousers and pants, then, still wearing his denim shirt, a favourite one with a fraying collar, he rests his weight on his elbows on either side of her and intrudes the head of his cock between her cunt lips. He holds himself very still, as still as she had been earlier, while her legs fall apart as wide as they will go and her feet draw up so that they are almost touching her buttocks; her calves and the backs of her thighs press tight together as she anticipates the glorious thrust. But he stays immobile, eyes searching hers, searching, and they both see something deep within the other which says all there is to say about everything, ever. Yet the exquisitely torturous need for that cock is the most powerful of her seething emotions and her lips move, she growls huskily, 'Fuck me. *Please*', and he says, 'Wait', and she says, 'No, *now. Do it'*.

Still he does not move, he drags the torture to intolerable limits and she insists through clenched teeth, *'Fuck me, damn it'*, and he suddenly slams into her with such force, ramming it right up to the hilt, his balls slapping into her buttocks, that he causes her to let loose a cry which is wholly primitive. Her knees pull back and she grips him with more power than her legs normally possess, her feet crossing on the small of his back as she tries to crush him, woman open to man as much as any woman could be.

They fuck like that with a consuming intensity, their every energy, physical and psychic, pours into that fucking which, at such a level, sexual gymnastics a poor relation, cannot last, they share the same, mind-wrenching orgasm, a series of explosions which drain their being, and they collapse.

A sublime exhaustion overtook Frannie's mind, she slid into a deep, brief sleep. When, fifteen minutes later, she opened her eyes, she found her lover at her side, propped on one elbow, studying her. 'Welcome back,' he said.

She rubbed a hand over her face. She smiled contentment. 'Sweet sleep,' she said.

'Me too, just a couple of minutes.' He had his trousers back on. Frannie looked down at herself; her bra, bedraggled, was draped around her neck, her blouse crumpled under her. When she started to straighten herself up he stopped her. 'I like to see you like that.'

She frowned at him. 'It's a touch blatant, isn't it?' The words coming from the mouth of another Frannie, whom she was just discovering. Frannie-in-love was not the same lusty Frannie who took perverse pleasure in such exposure. She stripped off the blouse and the bra. 'That's much better.'

Amused, he said, 'Sometimes I don't know what gives with you.'

'I'm not blatant any more. Just naked.'

'Oh.' He stared blankly at her.

'I love you, David, I really do.'

'Me too.'

She examined the palm of a hand, as if searching for words there. Then she said, carefully, 'I'm having – no, that's not right – *we're* having the most unbelievable orgasms together. I mean, I don't know if it's ever been quite like this before.'

'It's hard to believe not. You're married, you've probably had a lover or so in the meanwhile.'

She ignored the assumption. The truth would be too much for a man in love to cope with. 'Perhaps in the early days. Emotions are so hard to actually remember. But I don't think we make love any more. Not in the deepest sense.'

'But you love him?'

'Yes, I do.' She looked at him gravely. 'But nothing to do with what you and I have.'

'Is that eventually going to create a problem?'

She was quiet for some while, and began to pick at the hard skin under her big toe. This was not a question she wanted to face up to yet. It had already occurred to her and been shoved to the back of her mind. She found herself saying, 'I don't know David, I honestly don't know.' She could not look at him. 'It's – probable.'

'Oh.' Hollow.

'Please don't think about it now. Now we have each other, and your magic island to explore.'

He took a deep breath. 'Yes. I'm sorry. I guess I shouldn't have asked.'

'Maybe not. Never mind.' Finally she gave up her toe and looked at him. 'Why do you think that being in love adds so much to sex?'

He shrugged. 'Is there an answer to that? I've just been reading Norman Mailer's *Marilyn*. You know, about Marilyn Monroe? There's a line in there which stuck in my head. It's "Less is known about the true transactions of fucking than any science on earth".'

'Oh. Does that make sense?'

'When you consider, yes, it makes a powerful kind of sense. Take me, married and divorced twice, several mistresses, more one night stands than I care to remember. And every time it's different. At least, I think it was.'

'Never like this?'

'Something, I guess. I'm sure it was. I mean, it must have been. I've been in love. Totally consumed on four, five occasions. But when I look back, when I try to recall the feelings which were involved, all I remember are the faces, the physical acts and that it was damned good. You said emotions are hard to remember: Wrong: They're impossible to remember. Like taste or smell.'

'Yes. But what I get is, when I recall certain things which have happened to me, knowing that a powerful emotion of some sort was involved at the time, I get a – I don't really know even how to describe that – I get a sort of a nervous tension at the back of my throat, or in the pit of my stomach.'

'A confirmation that the emotion happened, but no

repetition of the feeling. That's the way it has to be 'of course. Imagine recalling different emotions one after the other. Fear, say, then sorrow, then love. You'd go nuts very quickly.'

'Maybe that's what happens to some mad people. Schizophrenics, for example. An unwanted gift of total recall.'

'Maybe.' He kissed her cheek and fondled her breast. Then he said, 'Enough of that. I suggest you get some clothes, we'll have a spot of lunch then I'll show you some of the island.'

After lunch he had her put on a loose skirt. He said he wanted to make love to her in one of his favourite magic places, but they would not be comfortable there naked.

He had a Range Rover, which got him to areas where no ordinary car could go. After ten minutes of driving they were clear of the grape plantation and heading through a plain surrounded by extinct volcanoes. It measured about six square miles, was completely flat and a kind of lichen gave it a rich green colour. In the middle of it he stopped so that Frannie could take a closer look. Where they stood, he explained, had once been a huge field of molten lava. It was covered with a network of cracks, from an inch to a foot wide and when Frannie dropped a stone into one of them she did not hear it hit the bottom. As she straightened up, David took her hand and led her a short way away from the car. 'Can you imagine that less than a hundred years ago, what we are walking on was white-hot and bubbling right down near the centre of the earth?' He pointed to a distant topless peak. 'That it shot out of that and poured down to fill this entire valley probably taking years to cool down and solidify. From the middle of the earth! What forces were released then, what power!' His eyes were shining.

Frannie found herself awed. She tried to imagine the

colossal event and the place where she was standing as being a white-hot, molten rock lake, and she was visited by the fleeting, chilling vision of herself sinking into it and being instantly, utterly consumed. Then she had a notion to feel it. She knelt down and flattened her hand on it; it was friendly, filled with the warmth of the afternoon sun. 'The very substance of being,' she murmured.

'A pretty idea, but no. Some sort of a relation, though. I guess the core of a planet has a special place in the order of things.'

'What an extraordinary thing! And all these cracks going down for ever.'

'As it cooled it contracted. Years of vibrant sound. A boiling, first, a bubbling sound filling the valley gradually calming down, quieter and quieter until, finally, a serene silence broken only by the occasional plop as the last of trapped gases found their way to the surface. Then a stillness for perhaps a year or so until the first tiny crack, which is followed by another and another, louder and louder until the whole air is alive with the pistol-sharp sounds of cracking rock, echoing around the hills and volcanoes. Can you *imagine*?'

She looked at him. 'You're amazing. You sound as if you were here.'

'Who knows? Perhaps I was.'

'Karma.' She felt infinitely small in this place. 'David,' she said softly, 'is this where you meant? You know, why I'm wearing a loose skirt?'

He smiled. 'No. This is only a part of the place. Come on.' Taking her elbow he helped her to her feet and they went back to the Range Rover.

They drove out of the lava lake and then through a small very white and clean town, where nobody seemed to be around except for a few old men standing outside bars or leaning against walls, who turned inscrutable eyes on them as they passed.

175

Ahead, Frannie saw what she took to be acre upon acre of ploughed clay field, but as they got closer she realized that they were approaching a new phenomenon. The clay was reddish rock, the biggest chunks of which were, from a distance, the ones which gave the impression of a ploughed field, and each was at least as big as a small car.

David stopped again so that she could examine the rock. Picking up a small chunk she found that it was porous and quite light, though its surface was scratchy. She clambered up onto one of the boulder-sized lumps and gazed around her; again a sea, a flat plain two or three miles across.

Back in the car as they drove along a road which had been bulldozed through the lava she said, '*This* was blown out of the ground? These massive rocks?'

'Yeah.'

'It's incredible. I can't believe it.'

'I can almost see it. Terrifying. The entire island must have been shaking from one end to the other.'

They drove in silence for a while, her hand resting lightly on his thigh. They came out of the lava field and David took a side-road. In fact it was hardly a road at all, merely a rough track which took them steadily upward on the foothills of a volcano. The track petered out and they were driving on what appeared to be hard-packed sand, but was actually a fine-grained volcanic ash of varying pastel shades.

They came to a stop on an almost level piece of ground and David got out. 'Come on.'

The view from there was astounding. Below them stretched the 'ploughed field', beyond it the smudge of town bouncing sunlight off its white walls, in the distance the lava lake, very green. That was the north. A few miles to the east across undulating, scrubby country, the Atlantic Ocean shimmered, and to the west was another sea, a sea of volcanoes, hills and craters, intensely beautiful, a mingling of soft colours which shifted through watery shades of blue and green and red and brown, lines and shapes both hard and gentle yet in perfect harmony under the almost cloudless sky. Above them, the slopes rearing up to it, was the crater from which had once belched the colourful ash on which they were standing.

Frannie found it almost unbearably beautiful. Her nostrils dilated as she savoured the freshness and the clean, sweet smell of the air.

'Listen,' said David.

'I don't hear anything.'

'You do. What you hear is nothing. You hear it very clearly.'

She tried again and was suddenly aware of what he meant. The silence was absolute. No birds, no insects, no breeze, not the slighest, tiniest sound. She *could* hear it. After a while she whispered. 'It's spooky.'

Just as quietly, David said, 'It's a powerful magic place.'

'This is *it*, then?' A constriction of her throat.

'This is the place, darling, yes.' There was a strange tension in his look. She had not seen him like that before, it was if the spot had found a way inside him. He took her by the elbows, gripping them hard. 'This is a place of sudden, violent death. It *is* dead. But it is both God and the Devil, in a weird reversal. Death above, here on the surface, life below, waiting to burst out again. The *power* here is immense.' His eyes were staring right into her. She could feel a vibrancy in his hands, some inner source of energy was surging from him to her through them.

'Take out my cock,' he said, and the simple words hit her being like a psychic punch.

No words. She dropped to her knees and fumbled his shorts undone, pulling down the elastic of his pants and his cock sprang out at her, filled with the

177

same throbbing force as his hands.

'Suck it.' An absolute order. Frannie down on her knees on the side of a volcano, sucking the cock of a man she loved, truly *sucking* on it as if trying to draw his essence out through it and into herself, while his hands knotted themselves in her hair, twisting and pulling, charged with a life and a need of their own.

Then he pushed her away, laid her down on her back on the warm lava ash, lifted her skirt, pulled the edge of her panties to one side and, no teasing play of the morning, thrust himself into her and *fucked* her and she *fucked* him back and when, quite soon, they approached their climax, he ordered her, 'Shout it out. *Scream* it out. Let the fucking *world* hear us', and she did and he did and the sound of their orgasms echoed and reechoed around the dead volcanic peaks, long after they themselves were silent, and Frannie was certain that she felt a rumbling from somewhere far below her.

Three miles away, a distant speck on the slopes of another volcano, a peasant riding a camel brought his beast to a stop and listened to the sounds, understanding what they were. His features remained immobile but a rare smile came to his eyes.

178

# 12
# Over – The Rainbow

David wanted to fuck her in each of his magical places and sometimes the practicability of this proved a little daunting. Such was the case in the caves known as the Jameos de Agua, in the north of Lanzarote.

When they arrived at the entrance to the caves, not on a mountain side or in a cliff but in a small depression in what was otherwise a monotonous, scrub-covered plain there were several cars and a tour bus parked nearby. David groaned – he had hoped to have the caves for themselves – but elected to go in anyway.

They were a series of interconnected, sometimes vast caverns, stretching far down into the earth and the magic here resided in the caves themselves and also in how man had intruded his contemporary personality into them with the use of light and sound, just as his early ancestors had with drawings. Subtle, pastel shades of light highlighted the extraordinary shapes, the rock pools, the massive stalactite and stalagmite formations. The music was all around Frannie and David as they made their way deeper and deeper within; more than quadrophonic, it seemed to pour out of the rugged walls on all sides and the roof, a strange mixture of composers and styles yet altogether fitting for the humbling experience of passing through underground spaces which were occasionally the dimensions of cathedrals. They would make their way silently through one of these caverns, just the two of them – the other visitors were swallowed up somewhere else – to the sound of Pink Floyd, duck through a narrow tunnel and emerge in another cavern where the baroque music of Vivaldi's *Four Seasons* filled the air. And when they reached a chamber which, because of its perfect accoustic balance was laid out and used as a concert hall, they were met by the powerful strains of Vangelis's *Heaven and Hell*.

In the cavern beyond the concert hall David led Frannie to a recess where there was a huge, natural hole in the wall, a man-made barrier across it. From there they had a view down to an underground lake, stretching in each direction as far as the eye could see, low lights playing on the water which still managed to give the impression of blackness, of timelessness.

David, his arm tight around Frannie, said, 'Impressive, no? And very deep. Right down there, where no light ever reached until recently, are to be found another of the wonders of the island.'

'What's that, darling?'

'Crabs, would you believe. Tiny crabs, completely blind, which are to be found in no other place in the world. Colourless and blind and believed by science to have evolved right there, down in that single lake. That's a heck of a thing to contemplate. In the depths of an island so much of which is dead, here are these crabs which seem to bear the very secret of life itself. Scientists from all over the world are intrigued but they haven't come up with any real answers. I mean, they didn't come here from anywhere, they simply happened.'

Frannie said nothing, staring down, trying to imagine how it was at the bottom of all that water. She felt David's hand move up from her waist and squeeze her breast, then it slid down to her buttocks and squeezed there, too, and she responded to the growing need in his touch, lifting her face to be kissed just as three other people, American tourists, joined them at the barrier. She was aware of his irritation at that in his kiss.

'Come on.' He led her away and back into the cavern. 'Over there.' She heard what he wanted to do in his voice and that, more than anything, made her want it too. A high rock jutted out of the ground, its face glowing pale orange, concealing a shadowy space between it and the cavern wall, which he backed her against. Taking her hand he put it flat against the crotch of his jeans; he was as hard as the rock behind her. But she could see the three Americans, two men and a woman, approaching them as he leant into her.

'Darling, people can see us,' she murmured.

'Not really. They see dark shapes, two people kissing perhaps. They can't quite make out what we are doing.' He paused. 'What we're going to do.'

She swallowed. 'Right here?'

'Right here. Close to those wonderful little blind creatures.' He put his hand down across hers, an insistent pressure. 'Get it out.'

She unzipped his jeans, pulled his pants down with one hand, and took hold of his cock with the other, sensitive to the fact that one of the American men was looking directly at them, a frown creasing his face, but even more aware of her own rising needs as she fisted his warm cock. She was wearing a loose, denim skirt which came to mid-thigh and no panties – his order of the day – and she had on tennis shoes. With his hands around her bare buttocks he hoisted her until their genitals were at the same level and, feet wrapped around the back of his calves, she found her own entrance with the tip of his cock and supressed the need to groan as he impaled her.

She could see over his shoulder up the slope of the

cavern to its access above that the Americans had gone. There was nobody else about. Resting his back against the rock which threw them into shadow, David began fucking her slowly and steadily, lifting her until his cock was almost free and using her own weight to let her slide down him until all of it was inside her, holding still like that for long seconds before repeating the process, while she made no movements of her own, immersed in letting him do it all to her.

She was beginning to build to a climax as somebody ducked out of the tunnel, followed by another, and another, a whole group of people, and David felt a sudden tension in her which had nothing to do with the fucking. 'What?' he said. He held her high, on the very tip of his cock.

'People. Lots of them.'

'I don't give a shit.' And he let her slide down, but quickly, dropping her, heaving her arse up again almost immediately, began to pull her on and off him like a man working out with a barbell, bringing silent gasps to her lips as her eyes watched the group of more than twenty tourists approaching and suddenly she didn't give a shit either, she was coming, he was coming and he flooded inside her, holding himself and her perfectly still as his cock pulsated and her cunt contracted in orgiastic spasms against it. She closed her eyes, her head dropped back and they stayed like that for long moments, then he hoisted her off his wet cock and let her gently down to the ground where she opened her eyes to discover that two elderly ladies had detached themselves from the group which was at the hole overlooking the lake and were slowly passing, no more than six feet away and fifteen seconds from her orgasm.

She smiled at them.

They were totally immersed in each other and in their

sex which they indulged all over his island. Her period came and went and they fucked right through it, leaving her blood on bed linen, a beach and the back seat of his Range Rover.

Then he wanted to have her in the sea, but with the perverse idea that there should be other people close by and he took her to the Playas Blancas, in the south, where everyone went naked. One reached the beaches by driving across country on very rough tracks. There was no bar or restaurant, and they took wine and ham and cheese and fresh crusty bread rolls.

They buried the two bottles up to their necks in sand where the sea washed over them, keeping the wine cool and after a primitive, satisfying lunch, both bottles consumed, heady with the alcohol and the sun and themselves, he walked her out to where the sea, swelling softly, covered their waists, and they fucked standing up in front of a beach with a hundred people looking on.

Afterwards, they stretched luxuriously out side by side. Frannie said, 'Do you think anyone knew what we were doing?'

He laughed. 'Sure. It was pretty obvious, I should have thought. Two naked people locked in each other's arms for that long in the sea.'

'I wonder if it turned any of them on?'

'At least three it sure did. At a certain point they rolled onto their bellies. But they swivelled around so that they could still watch us.'

'Dirty bastards.'

They slept for a while, then they read. He was reading the works of William Blake and he interrupted her Scott Fitzgerald – she was into *The Great Gatsby* for the second time – at the crucial point where the gardener sees Wilson's body lying in the grass.

'Can I read something to you?'

'Of course.'

'It seems to be appropriate to the moment. Listen. "The pride of the peacock is the glory of God. The lust of the goat is the bounty of God. The wrath of the lion is the wisdom of God. The nakedness of women is the work of God".'

Frannie grinned. 'What's most appropriate? The lust of the goat?'

His eyes travelled her body. 'I was more thinking of the last.'

'Thanks.' She was lying on her stomach, back arched, chin cupped in hands, facing the sea. 'Is that also the work of God? If so he didn't do a very good job.'

He followed her gaze. A nude woman, a mountain of flesh burnt a raw pink, was emerging from the sea and with each step it seemed that every inch of her gross body shuddered. A green plastic bathing cap covered in coloured plastic flowers contrived to make the obscene appear ridiculous.

'That *is* something else, isn't it? There ought to be a law against people like that walking around naked.' He glanced at his book. 'Actually, that little piece *was* from Proverbs of Hell.'

'Thanks a *lot*.'

He laughed briefly, then he stared at her for long moments, at her wonderfully supple naked body, the skin tanned a gentle golden hue, hair damp and sticky with salt yet still managing to allure as it draped over her shoulders. The thought came to him that much of his semen was still inside her, and then another thought came into his head, and it jolted him. He said, 'I'm not sure if I could live without you.'

Frannie said, thinly, 'Oh.'

'Is that all you can say? You know how I feel.'

'Yes, I …' She took a slow, deep breath. Suddenly being forced to think, she found she did not want to. They had been almost three weeks together, incredible

184

weeks, she was in love, there could hardly be any doubt about that and her rare thoughts of Victor, thoughts tinged with guilt because sex was what she was supposed to be seeking, not love, had been stuffed into the back of her mind like a trunk in an attic. She looked at David from beneath lowered lashes, this superstar, this gypsy-souled David Donnelly who had staked a claim to her being. And she didn't know what to say.

'Do you love me?'

'I love you. I tell you fifty times a day.'

'Tell me again.'

'I love you.'

'Will you marry me?'

The words jolted her. She looked down at the upside-down, open cover of *Gatsby*. 'That's a terribly complicated question.'

'I don't see why. We love each other. We get married. Clear and simple.'

'Clear and simple it is not, David. You seem to forget, I *am* married.' Her finger traced an 'o' in the sand.

'You get a divorce. That's simple enough.'

'Not.'

'What?'

She searched her inner self, finding little but confusion. Then she said, 'I'm sorry David, I'm not that sure if I want a divorce.'

'But that's a contradiction.' His voice was becoming toneless as he experienced a rising fear.

She looked at him. Pain. 'No, it's not.' She shrugged. 'I love him, he's my husband, he adores me. I don't know if I can do it to him.'

'Not even for *me*? For our love?' He rested a hand on the back of her leg. 'You must? Surely you must.'

'Must I? Look, I have to think. I have to think very deeply.'

He shook his head. 'There's not that much time. I have to go off to Australia to make a movie in a couple of weeks. I want you with me.'

This was news. She suddenly remembered her own approaching obligation in that direction. She was not going, of course. She had not the slightest interest any more. Of course. But he was off to Australia. She said, 'How long will you be?'

'It's a big one. Six months.'

'And you want me to come and live with you in Australia for six months?'

'Of course I do. And for you to get a divorce organised at the same time.'

'Oh.' The headiness of her love for him somehow did nothing to stop her feeling that she was being asked to make a dramatic decision far too quickly.

'Look, maybe I can't afford Lear jet runabouts for you, but I'm still a very wealthy man.'

'Darling, don't be silly.' Abruptly she turned around and sat up, noticing as she did so a couple out there in the sea who might have been doing the same as they had done earlier; but she was too involved in the turmoil in her head to take more than the most fleeting interest. 'You think I care about money that much?'

'I don't know. You live about the richest life-style I've come across.'

'Do I?' She thought about that, so much of which she took entirely for granted. Maybe she would miss her jet, her castle. There was no doubt about her ongoing love affair with Stratton Castle, with its history, its magnificence. Victor, and their principal home, were a most important part of her life on which it would be difficult to turn her back. Even for David. Even for their love. She said, 'Perhaps I do, but that's hardly the point,' thinking as the words left her mouth that perhaps it was, at least, a part, of the point.

'Okay. What is, then?'

'Whether or not I want to totally change my life.'

'But you must,' he insisted, feeling a very real dread at the unthinkable possibility of losing her.

'Oh, shit.' She looked unhappily at him. 'How can I tell you what I feel when I don't know myself? Look, maybe it's something like this. I've got two sorts of love. There's you, this. Explosive, instantaneous. Emotions which knock us right off our feet. And there's my husband. Old, comfortable love, like a well-worn pair of slippers. Won't hurt me. And you're forcing me to choose.' She paused, a possibility occuring to her. 'Why can't I have both?'

'For Christ's sake. How can you have both?'

'I'll see you again when your film's finished. I'll even spend some time there with you in Australia. My husband and I have an understanding. We ...'

He interrupted her. 'You didn't tell me that. That sort of crap is in itself one step away from a divorce.'

'No, it isn't. You couldn't possibly understand. Our relationship is perhaps more consumed with sex than other people's.' She was going to leave it at that but something drove her on. 'We've been married eight years and during that time we've taken our sex lives beyond normal limits. You know, threesomes, sex parties, that sort of thing.'

He was staring at her with an expression which said, *This I don't want to hear*. 'That's the British upper classes?'

'No. But it's me. And it's Victor. We sort of thrive on it, I suppose.'

'My God.'

'But there's nothing wrong with it. It works for us. I mean, he'll be delighted to know I'm having a wonderful time with you.' She paused in order to let this revelation sink in. Then she went on, carefully. 'But he'll be crushed, David, by my falling in love with you, by my leaving him for you.'

187

'It sounds as if he ought to be crushed. With a road roller.' Bitterness.

'Don't be unfair.'

'I think you're being unfair. To us.'

'I haven't said no to you David.' Appeasement. She could only just bear what she was doing to him, she was doing it to herself as well.

'Pretty fucking close to it, I'd say.'

'Give me another week?'

A failed attempt at a smile. 'Okay.'

Silence.

Propped on one elbow, watching him sleep. Just a sheet over his big chest, it rises and falls with gentle precision. Frannie thinking. 'He is so beautiful, such a lovely, lovely man. How can I let it end, loving him like this? My gypsy. But I must, I have to. It won't last for ever, he'll tire of me. Not Victor. With Victor I have something for life. Lady Ballington. I *like* being Lady Ballington. I don't want to lose that. But I want you as well, David I want you desperately. Let me have both?'

The two of them sitting on a patch of grass on some black rocks, a line of small cliffs, the sea twenty feet below them. The sea lazily powerful, long, deep, swells starting way out, breaking at the last moment. Every so often one of the waves catching the entrance to a narrow cave below them in such a way that it collides with a surge of water backing out and there is a hollow, strident *wump* which echoes, a mist of spray is thrown up high above the cliff edge and the rays of the sun fragment through it into a rainbow.

They have been there half an hour, drinking beer, and they have come to recognize a pattern in the waves, know with which oncoming rush of water this rainbow will happen. It is another, trivial, magic of the island, too soft to be dramatic but evocative of fine feelings.

He destroys her reverie. 'Today's a week, Frannie.'

She knows what he means. She sighs. 'Yes.'

'You promised.'

'I did, didn't I?'

'Well, who's it to be? Me or Victor?' She can hear how he is trying to keep the shake out of his voice.

'Must it be like that? Must I be faced with such a choice? Can't we have what I believe Americans call an ongoing affair?'

'I want to *marry* you, Frannie. I won't share you with somebody else. I can't.'

'It's easy for you. You only have us to consider. I have two of you.'

'I want you to choose.'

Resentment as she thinks, 'Of course you do. Male Macho Movie Actor'. She knows this is unfair. 'Give me a few more days? Please?'


'*I'll* marry him like a shot,' said Matilda.

They were sitting on the terrace of Matilda's Arrecife hotel room. 'Must you make light of everything?' said Frannie.

'What else? I thought you were too intelligent to be acting like a love-sick cow. Whatever that may be.'

'I have two days to decide. Then he's off. *If* he goes when I say no.'

'When, I believe, is the operative word. You didn't say if.'

Frannie gave her a look which was infinitely sad. 'No. I didn't, did I?'

'No. You know where you belong and so do I. Sooner or later you'll break with this man in any case. You've had your fill, it's time to get it over with.'

'My *fill*? I haven't had my fill, damn it! It's not like that. Oh, Christ, I can't stand this.' Tears welled and trickled down her cheeks as she stared with blank, unseeing eyes over the broad expanse of Arrecife beach.

'I need to shop for a few women's bits and pieces. Gregory's picking me up shortly in a taxi.' She succeeds in keeping her voice normal.

'I'd have taken you into town.'

'I didn't want to bore you with it.'

He is tense. 'Listen, you still haven't given me an answer. I'm due to leave the day after tomorrow. Oh, *fuck it*! This is fucking *killing* me.' He grips her elbow, too hard. 'You *have* to give me an answer, you hear?'

She does not look at him. She can't. 'Please? You're hurting me.'

'Sorry.' He lets go. He has no more words, all arguments are exhausted, it is only up to her.

She hears the taxi draw up, is relieved but at the same time filled with a dread which threatens to suffocate her. 'I'll see you in a little while,' she lies, and she turns her back on him and walks quickly out of the house.

David Donnelly, close to despair, watched her go. Never having given quite as much of himself to a woman as he had to Frannie, his need was desperate. Going out into his cacti and lava garden, he watched the blue, ten year old Mercedes cab as it travelled fast through the black and green vineyards, until it shrank to a spot in the distance and disappeared. Then he returned to his house and descended into his lava bubbles. It felt desolate in there; without her presence the house seemed to have died. He did not understand why the sensation should happen so suddenly, be so pressing, but his gypsy soul told him that it was to let him know that something was terribly wrong.

He was drawn into the bedroom, where the jean shorts and denim shirt that she had changed out of to go to town were lying casually on the bed, and that perfectly ordinary sight imparted a foreboding, a sense of finality. He inspected the wardrobe. All the clothes she had brought to the house hung neatly there but again, they disturbed him in the weirdest way. In the drawers, her underwear. On an impulse he scooped up a handful of panties and buried his nose in them, then dropped them as the woman-smell caused him a pain of loss which was beyond his understanding. He looked around. Apart from the shorts and the shirt, everything was in its place.

Then his eyes found it. Intruding for no more than an eighth of an inch from the coverlet on his bed. A tiny corner of white paper. A sickness of fear turned cruelly on him then. He knew it was an envelope. He knew that there would be a note inside that envelope. Worst of all, he knew what it would say. It was more than a minute before he could summon the courage to take it from under the coverlet.

*David* on it in a neat hand which strangely enough he had never before seen. In his hand it felt heavy with the words he knew it contained. Then, a moment's savagery, he ripped it open, tearing the top of the paper inside as he did so. The note. Oh, so simple few words packing a Sonny Listen slug to the soul.

*My darling, more talking is useless. It has to be like this. I'm truly sorry, my gypsy. Your only satisfaction may be that these words are tearing me apart as I write them. I love you, will always. Goodbye.*

He read it once only, then, trembling with an inner rage which, as it built, threatened to explode against the entire world, he screwed the paper into a tight ball and hurled it across the room. He bellowed, an awesome mingling of rage and despair and fear, rushed from the room, dragged himself up the spiral staircase and out into the sunlit island which was as dark as a gathering storm. Leaping behind the wheel of his Land Rover he gunned it away in a furious panic. The old couple, who had heard his subterranean roar from the garden, watched without expression as the car slewed out into the road and screamed through the gears.

But by the time he reached Arrecife Airport, the Lear jet was out on the runway, gathering momentum for take-off.

Helpless, defeated, he could only watch as the elegant plane left the ground and soared off towards the sea. Frannie did not see him. She was leaning back in her seat, eyes closed, fighting back her tears.

# 13
# My Lady Lost And Lonesome

She did not know where to go, in which corner of the world she would be free of him. There was no place, of course, but that did not stop her from searching for it.

She had directed her pilot to fly to Malaga. She had a half-formed idea of returning to the hospitality of the Litford's, but when the plane taxied to a halt on the scorched July tarmac she realized that Las Brisas, or for that matter anywhere she had spent time with David was going to damage her with its memories, rubbing salt into very open wounds. Even Malaga Airport itself held bitter-sweet vibrations. She was impatient to refuel and get away from there.

They went north to Shannon in Ireland, where the Lear would be topped up with fuel once again. During the three hour flight Frannie tried to come to terms with her mind which was agonising over what she had done. Lady Ballington and her jet were heading through limbo at five hundred miles an hour.

She tried watching a movie for a while, which only irritated her; watching Paul Newman did nothing to take her mind off her own movie star. She had Matilda stop it. As she sat down, Matilda said, 'You've hardly spoken a word to me. Let me help.'

Frannie turned listless eyes to the window. 'I doubt if you can.'

'I can try. I just think you ought to hear from somebody who cares about you that you've done the only thing possible. You *had* to break your romance up.' She paused, looking earnestly at the back of Frannie's head. 'You do love Victor, don't you?'

There was a long silence. Frannie twisted her head, looked at Matilda with flat eyes. 'Yes, I love Victor.'

'And he you. It's the only thing which matters.'

'Is it?'

'Most certainly. Okay, you've had a wonderful, magical fling. But now it's over. Like a rather super holiday – sad when it comes to an end but the end has to be faced up to.'

'I wish it were as easy. God, it's awful. And what I must have done to *him*.'

'He'll get over it. His world is inhabited by gorgeous, nubile young therapists.'

Frannie managed a rueful smile. 'It is, isn't it? But he'll be hurting too much for that.'

'For a while, perhaps. But then that's what he'll do. He'll screw you out of his system. That's what his sort of man always does.'

'Perhaps.'

'And another thing. I believe that love at first sight is a myth. Not that something of the sort doesn't appear to happen, but the myth is in its lasting value. Those situations inevitably have sticky endings. Love which comes in with a bang goes out with a bang.'

'You succeed in being extraordinarily vulgar at times.'

Matilda grinned. 'I didn't mean it quite like that. Well, thank God you haven't lost your dirty mind.'

Frannie raised an eyebrow, said nothing. Matilda was finding the tiniest chink in her armour of depression.

'You've got out at the right time for both of you. No, for the three of you. And Victor's love, unusual as it may be, is a love that's grown. Your love for him, too. He married your seventeen year old body and you married money and a title. Now, your relationship, albeit with its amazing sexual licence, is powerful enough to give you the strength to tear yourself away from your great love.'

'Were it not for Victor I would probably have been Mrs Donnelly already.'

'And a sadder, wiser, ex-Mrs Donnelly in a while, I'll guarantee.'

'Maybe.'

'So. Where are we going after Shannon? I'd just like to know how many more of these terrifying take-offs and landings I have to endure.'

'Sorry.' She took hold of Matilda's arm. 'I really don't know where to go next. Oh, shit, Matilda I'm really quite lost.'

'Then why don't we go home? Back to Stratton?'

'And take my mess back to Victor? No, I don't think so. That's hardly fair. I've got to get sorted out first.'

'Mmmm. Like David you'll need therapy.'

Frannie sighed. 'I don't think I can face the idea of letting myself get picked up. Of getting laid by somebody else.'

'That's understandable.' Matilda thought for a moment. 'But, surely, wasn't there something about a part in a sex film?'

Frannie looked blankly at her. 'There was. You know, I'd quite forgotten.'

'Why don't you do it? Help take your mind off David, I should think.'

Frannie considered. It had nothing to do with that other type of sex, of getting picked up, of insincere pretending to fancy the man, of fucking which would be, the way she felt at present, distasteful because she would be trying to imagine the man was David. It had to do with the mechanics of being screwed on camera by several different men, following a script, being under instruction, the whole strangely compelling

195

scene. A vigorous, daily, on-camera fucking. The more she thought about it, the more the idea began to appeal, making some sort of mad sense. Also it began to produce in her the mildest of erotic stirrings and when she realized this she knew that that was what she was going to do.

She went into the cockpit and had her pilot plan his course ahead for the long trip to California.

# 14
# Making Movies

It was a subdued, nervous, unhappy Frannie who, four days later, entered Bernard Goldberg's studios for Day One of the shooting. The absence of David, the need for him, had proved an almost intolerable burden.

During her first breakfast in the Beverly Hills's Hotel, she had opened a newspaper to find herself face-to-face with a picture of him arriving at Melbourne and the sight of him caused her physical pain. He had lost weight, his cheeks were drawn and he appeared thoroughly miserable; his smile for the camera was clearly contrived.

Only the Pacific Ocean separated them and the temptation to take her plane across it to him had been almost overwhelming, resisted only because of Matilda's help.

The first person she met that morning was Tony, and he seemed as mentally off as she was. It appeared that something dramatic must have happened to him, too, since last she saw him on stage in Amsterdam. He was almost unfriendly with her, avoiding her eyes, offering no explanation why.

But he fucked her all right, Tony could always be depended upon to get it up in public.

It was a porno film with the thinnest of story-lines involving an orgy at a fancy dress party at the beach-front house of a millionaire Arab one evening

197

and night, some of the guests carrying on their sex the following afternoon at sea on the Arab's yacht. In it, Frannie was dressed as a medieval queen, except that medieval queens did not wear garter belts and stockings and neither, presumably, did they wear see-through knickers from Bonnie Keller. She was a masked queen, to start with, and the donning of the mask brought back vivid memories of her twisted night in Amsterdam.

She was to be the first of the females to be screwed. As she was told what was expected of her she had an urge to run from there, finding herself on the wrong side of cold indifference, only able to think of David and what his reaction would be were he to know what she was doing. But she stayed.

It was supposed to be after a *Tom Jones* style gluttonous feast, that was to be shot some other time. Filming started with a space being cleared across the middle of the banquet table and Frannie was bent over it, her shoulders pinned by a man in a bear-suit, facing her while a devil behind her, Tony, lifted her voluminous skirts high up her back and dropped her knickers whilst another girl on her knees, Nell Gwynn, gave him head.

Frannie experienced no sexual stirrings at first, as her knickers were removed, and she proved too dry for Tony to enter her comfortably. They had to cut while she, remaining exposed like that in front of camera crew and actors was lubricated with baby oil by Tony as Goldberg voiced his impatience. But once Tony was into her, ramming it in to Goldberg's machine-gunned instructions, the situation began to take an inevitable hold on her, her own juices started to flow into the oil and when the bear-man unzipped his artificial coat, produced his cock and intruded it into her mouth, those two cocks going to work on her completed the job of unfreezing her, and thoughts of David faded into haze as her mind became absorbed in what was happening to her body.

The Nell Gwynn girl strutted moodily around the table, hands on hips and when she reached the bear man she shoved him away with a contemptuous laugh, lifting her skirts and thrusting her bared cunt lewdly at Frannie's face.

Apart from Matilda this is the first female Frannie has had sexual contact with in a long while. She grasps her buttocks, clutching the plump flesh with relish as her tongue pushes its way inside a cunt which is framed with a delicate fuzz of the lightest brown hair, begins to work steadily up and down in rhythm with Tony's energetic pounding and slides the tip of a finger into the girl's tight little arsehole. Another girl, black tail-coat, velvet bow tie, nothing else, is laid back next to Frannie and fucked by the bear man. While this happens to her she watches Frannie eating cunt and reaches deep down the crack of Frannie's arse to where she can touch Tony's thrusting prick. Two cameras, one still, one moving in and around while Goldberg hovers, non-stop instructions, Frannie now so abandoned she is only barely aware of off-set action as she tastes sweet juice and Tony's fucking builds her up towards a climax.

Tableaux do not keep the same formation for long in a Goldberg epic. Frannie is turned over, supine, her head hangs back over the edge of the table, Tony's place is taken by a black man in a white suit whose first thrust with a huge cock brings a gasp to her lips. The Nell Gwynn girl moves on and Tony is there, fucking her inverted face, full balls slapping against her nose.

Frannie comes, the cock in her mouth stifling her moans, but the fucking goes on. Each of five men have a go at her in various positions across that table and as the black man's cock stretches her mouth, as someone else who she can't see – but it makes no difference –

199

Vaselines her arse and buggers her, another climax rushes up on her and, feeling as if her whole body has been turned into a cunt, she comes again, animal sounds, as she licks the black man's balls.

The cameras stop rolling for a short while, the fucking comes to a halt but the men stand around holding their cocks, keeping them up, while Frannie is undressed by a crew assistant, a little gay boy and, in suspenders and stockings she is positioned by Goldberg on her side on the table, nose to crotch, sixty-nine, with the tailcoat girl who now only wears the bow. Eager for this seventeen year old cunt, Frannie savours it for a full minute before the cameras roll again.

Six men, among them Tony and the black man, arrange themselves on either side of the table, wanking, ogling the girls as they eat each other, Goldberg urging them to *finish* it, to *toss* off those pricks, and Tony is the first to come. He is standing across the table from Frannie's buried head and as he begins to shoot Goldberg shouts, 'Lift the head, Frannie! Lift it!' The words register almost too late, as Tony's first two vigorous spurts spray over Frannie's shoulder and the bow-tie girl's arse, but he has a third and Frannie takes it full in the face, opening her mouth, getting some in there then sticky with it she dives back to the cunt, feeling gloriously dirty as she pushes Tony's cum inside with her tongue. One by one, the men shoot over the girls, the last to come the black man who drenches both of their bellies and Frannie savours his spunk from Bow-Tie's navel.

Goldberg calls cut and Bow-Tie immediately rolls away from Frannie to the floor, and hurries off to clean herself up. But Frannie, cum from six cocks over her face, in her mouth, her hair, over her back, her tits, her arse, her thighs, wallowing in it, is too far gone into her third orgasm to leave it at that. She lies on her back and,

200

totally unaware of the professional activity around her, she masturbates herself into a frantic climax which she shouts at the ceiling. Then she lies still.

Goldberg, observing this final, unrecorded act with impassive eyes, says, 'You were great, Frannie. Just great.'

She cannot wait for each day's shooting to begin. David, still longed for and pined over in the evenings, shares his memories with those of the day's sexual happenings and with thoughts anticipating the erotic events of the day to come, and with her body and mind well-used and weary she sleeps easily, dreaming usually not of her deserted love but of yet more sex.

By Day Eight of the filming more than half of the unedited video-tape in the can. When she is not required on set until the following morning, she shows up anyway to watch the action, much of it on a facsimile of a grand staircase, and four times during the course of that day she disappears to masturbate.

She has received Tony's cock on more than a dozen occasions when the final day arrives, but apart from that he has remained uncommunicative and distant towards her which continues to puzzle her.

The closing scene was the final one of the yacht where almost everyone concerned with the previous action, all of them naked, had got to screw everyone else. Goldberg contrived a near-impossible contortion in the last tableau, choosing Frannie as the star. It took him almost a half an hour to set this up to his satisfaction, Frannie meanwhile on knees and elbows getting terribly cramped and frustrated, being filled with cocks, handling two as the men lay lengthwise on the gently rolling ship facing her, her elbows placed as far apart as they would go so that two more men could kneel in front of her, facing her, their calves positioned beneath the lying couple, slowly masturbating their swollen cocks inches from her mouth while the black man, beneath her, kept his cock still in her cunt as Tony inserted his into her arse. For a while Frannie reexperienced the torments of the magazine photo sessions but finally they were all banging into her and she forgot her stiffness; fucking and sucking and wanking with abandon until one by one they came over her, sperm hitting her all over. Tony was the last, pulling out of her arse and shooting over her back. She came herself then, a series of little, pulsating explosions and, as Goldberg pronounced the final 'cut' of the picture, she wantonly smeared and mingled the men's semen over her flesh, rubbing it in, licking final drops from her fingers, from around the edges of her mouth. Then she climbed shakily to her feet, clambered over the ship's rail and let herself flop into the warm waters of the Pacific.

A little later, as they were berthing in a nearby marina, Tony approached her. His attitude towards her was the same as it had been during the entire two weeks – hesitant, reluctant – but he surprised her by saying, 'Listen, er, Frannie, a few of the technical boys were thinking of getting together a little sex party of their own with one or two of the girls. I'm invited. Fancy coming along?'

She looked puzzlement at him. 'I thought you were right off me.'

'Oh, did you?' He was not looking at her, he was watching the little gay boy help drop rubber fenders.

'You've hardly said two words to me in all this time. Which I find surprising to say the least in view of our, er, activities.'

'Oh. Yeah, well I guess, I guess I'm not in a talkative mood.'

'You can say that again.'

'I'm not in a talkative mood.' He turned to her, sounding a touch angry. 'Look, Frannie, I'm asking you to a goddamn small suburban party, that's all. No big deal. I'll run you out.'

'Thanks. I haven't said I'd come.'

The annoyance disappeared, he even sounded a bit anxious. 'You *will* come, won't you?' Something in his eyes seemed wrong; to Frannie his eyes didn't match his voice.

She looked away. Two men in white on the dock were helping to make the yacht fast. 'I'll think about it,' she said. 'But if I do Gregory takes me. I'll pick you up.'

'Always Gregory, huh?'

'Always Gregory.'

'Well, why not? What time?'

A gathering breeze gusted hair over her eyes. Holding it back she said, 'I haven't agreed yet.'

He was irritated again. 'Come on. I have to know now.'

She frowned at him. 'What's all this big urgency?'

'It's tomorrow night. If you won't do it I need to organise another chick.' Putting his hand on her waist he pronounced words which the tone of his voice belied. 'Please? For old times sake? I *want* it to be with you. We never did get it together without a camera around.'

'But there'll be people in any case. You said it was a sex party.'

He placed a kiss on the tip of her nose, but it felt all wrong. 'We can slip off alone together, find an empty room.' He paused. 'Well. Are you coming?'

It was inexplicable, she was getting contradictory, very peculiar vibrations from him. But, perversely, she chose to ignore them. She seemed to have gone some small way to screwing David out of her system, she was not over-keen for the screwing to stop.

So she said yes.

203

# 15
# A Nest Of Jackals

A wide, clean street, one of a chequered maze of similar streets in sprawling suburban Los Angeles. Unassuming. Elm trees in tidy rows with grass verges separating them, low, fresh-painted wooden fences, neat front lawns, Wistaria, square brick bungalows each differing, but not a lot, from its neighbour. Middle Management homes for Mr Average America. Unthreatening.

Gregory brought the Cadillac Eldorado to a stop under a street lamp. There was a short drive to the house but it was filled with two cars and the gates were shut. There was a party going on in the house next door, windows were open and the garden was bathed in music and light. In contrast, this house was gloomy, no sign of life but for a dull glow from behind heavy brown curtains.

Frannie, somewhat tipsy, was hot for whatever was coming to her. Almost two weeks of heavy screwing in front of video cameras might have jaded another girl's appetite, but not for Frannie. During the last ten minutes of the drive Tony's big, insatiable cock had been in her mouth, she was deliciously warm between her legs, and the crotch of her Christian Dior, crêpe de chine knickers was damp.

Tony experienced a little difficulty in zipping himself up; his hard-on was threatening to burst out of his tailored slacks as he got out of the car. Gregory, from the front seat, followed their progress with eyes which were unamused as they went through a pointed wooden gate, along a crazy paving path lined with rose trees and Frannie rang a bell beside a green-painted front door with square, opaque panes of glass from top to bottom. There was a four-toned chime.

They were let in by a swarthy, middle-aged man in a black leather suit whom Tony introduced as John, a lighting technician on the film. Frannie did not recognize him, but then there had been a number of faces in and around the sets over the days and her big preoccupation had been sex. He took them into a drab room whose only character was its bad taste: three china ducks were in flight across one, flower-papered wall, a small round mirror on another was framed with a collection of large gilt points, and brown curtains clashed with a deep-blue three-piece suite. Another man, thirty, in a denim suit, got up as they entered. Tony introduced him as Ingram, a cameraman, and Frannie failed to recognize him, as well. With an oily smile he apologised casually about the room. It was, he explained, a rented house.

Having been surrounded by video equipment for two weeks, it did not occur to Frannie to wonder about the camera lying on a sideboard or the arc lamps standing in two corners of the room. This was, in any case, supposed to be a party for film crew.

Tony said, 'We're a bit early. The others will be along in a little while.' His voice sounded flat and she noticed that he had lost his hard-on.

Something certainly felt wrong. The only sounds resembling a party were drifting in from next door. And she did not much care for Ingram's smarmy looks although John seemed all right. But the warmth and taste of Tony's cock was still in her mouth; she had turned herself on in the car and she was tipsy. She ignored the little warning signs which her subconscious was picking up. Ingram drowned out next door with a tape, Frank Sinatra, 'Nancy with the Laughing Face', too loud on a simple radio-cassette, distorting, while John fixed her a vodka and orange.

It started quite quickly, John put out the overhead light and the room became softer, if not less drab, illuminated with a glow from behind the china ducks. Frannie, vaguely wondering when the other girls were going to show, settled back in the sofa with Tony, the powerful Polish vodka in her drink hitting what was already inside her, making her woozy as they made small talk, Ingram on a pouffe, John astride a reversed upright chair, leaning on its back.

When Tony's hand slid under her pencil slim, coteline dress, they all stopped talking. There was suddenly a tense expectancy in the air, and she allowed the hand to continue on its way as he whispered. 'Why wait for the others?' Finding the edge of her panties he got a finger under it and into her as with the other hand he began to undo her dress which had buttons down its front, starting at the bottom.

Letting herself go in this situation, to ride with it, was easy for Frannie.

She had been screwed by so many men in the last fortnight, with plenty more, including, presumably John and Ingram although she did not remember them looking on, that it had become second nature to her. The more buttons Tony undid the wider she spread her legs, as she watched John tilting forward on his chair, eyes, eyes which lacked expression, narrowing as he looked on. But then, strangely, when she went for Tony's zipper, he pushed her hand away, quite brusquely, not before she discovered that customary, instant erection had failed to occur. He kissed her, his lips cold; again, something not quite right in that, and

206

in his eyes, but she was far gone with all her buttons undone and two fingers right up her. She wriggled against the fingers and began slowly closing and opening her silk-stockinged legs.

Ingram got up and stood over them, watching. Then, saying nothing, he unzipped his jeans and got out of them, and stripped off his pants. With only half a hard-on, he knelt next to Frannie on the sofa, hanging his drooping cock over Frannie's face. For Frannie he was now only a cock, and the oiliness of his face was unimportant. She took him inside her mouth and, as he grew there, as Tony worked her knickers down and off with one hand, she began to lose herself in her first non-instructed orgy in several weeks.

But Tony – Tony had lost the apparent enthusiasm he had shown during the car ride. Her knickers in his hand, he suddenly got up and walked away, dropping them on the table while Frannie, busy with Ingram's cock, failed to see the look of anger which he flashed at John. Putty, she let herelf be pulled to her feet and bent over the back of the sofa. As Ingram got his cock in her and began to screw her with long, determined thrusts – yet another cock beginning to bring her to orgasm – as Sinatra flew to his Moon, John, who had been busying himself with the two arc-lamps switched them on, the flood of light momentarily blinding Frannie. He said in a matter-of-fact voice. 'We thought it might be interesting to make a little amateur film of the action.'

Outside, Gregory was thirsty. The hired Cadillac carried no drinks, but he remembered passing a bar a few streets back which had looked convivial and inviting. Lord Ballington's instructions had been never to leave his post, but this occasion, Gregory considered, was different, since Frannie was safe with someone she knew very well. In any case, the bar was close by. He started the engine, engaged drive and rolled away from the house.

Frannie was far too engrossed in this new sexual situation to let the lights do anything but momentarily distract her, and she was close to being drunk. John moving in with his camera was no more than a repetition of what had been happening to her every day on set. In fact it was an added, special kick, and she performed for it with enthusiasm, allowing herself to be laid on her back on the carpet and fucked and filmed like that, coming very close to climax but not making it because she was pulled to her feet and taken to the old, heavy oak table on which lay her knickers, Ingram stripping her naked before laying her back on it, holding her hands above her head, pumping into her again.

And she failed to notice that John had put his camera aside and in its place was a length of rope, and that the door had opened and another man had entered. She was unaware of anything wrong until the moment when her hands, already restrained at the wrists by Ingram, were seized, one by John, the other by the newcomer, thin ropes were curled around her wrists and she began to scream, a scream quickly stifled as her own Christian Dior knickers were stuffed into her mouth; her hands, wide apart, were tightly secured to the tops of the table legs.

The newcomer walked slowly around the table as Ingram uncoupled from her. He stood at her knees, a leer on his face, then he rammed two fingers viciously up her cunt, hurting her, his fingernails scratching. He said, 'Good evening, my dear Lady Ballington.'

It was Prinsen, the Dutchman, the sex-show operator from Amsterdam.

# 16
# No Sympathy For The Devil

The almost invisible hairs on her spine stood on end. Too stunned to think, Frannie stared in incomprehension at the Dutchman as her legs were spread and her ankles secured to the table. She heard Tony muttering, 'Oh my God, I'm sorry,' and the Dutchman told him to shut his fucking mouth.

Prinsen placed two knotted fists on either side of Frannie's thighs and leant towards her. 'You know what you *did* to me, Lady Ballington? You know what your lunk of a chauffeur *did* to me?' Evil threaded through his too-calm delivery. 'His blow caused me a blindness, I am being blind in one eye. My friend, Danny, he shattered his jaw in eleven places. It is wired up for weeks yet.' He mouthed a grin, flat, infinitely chilling, and fear shuddered through her. 'So. These things you are not getting away with.' He spat on her belly.

She began to function through her terror, found she could reach her emerald with her thumb. It was difficult to manoeuvre, but with effort she managed its half-turn.

The bleeper sounded. But it went unheard. It was not in Gregory's top pocket, but was lying in the glove compartment of the car. Gregory's head was tilted back as he poured ice-cold Schlitz beer down his throat.

The Dutchman stared between Frannie's wide open

legs. 'A very fucked cunt, I understand from friend Tony.' He contemplated, thin lips twisted in a crooked smile.

'They threatened to kill me, Frannie.' From Tony.

'Shut your mouth,' said Prinsen. 'That is true, of course. We would have killed him. What poor Tony is thinking is that all you are to get is a severe beating. What is happening is that this' – he unzipped his trousers and took out a hard cock – 'this is to be the last prick you will ever know, dear Frannie.'

Tony gasped. 'Shit, *no!*' Sinatra ran out of steam and next door's party invaded the room. Frannie's ears strained for sounds of Gregory – he should have been with her by now. Her terror mounted as she heard none.

Taking his time about it, the Dutchman fished a black silk hood from his pocket and rolled it over his head so that she saw only his glinting eyes. 'Get the film rolling, John,' he said through the silk. Using both hands he opened her cunt, stared at it for several seconds, then thrust in his cock. 'Enjoy your last fucking.' Her buttocks were overlapping the table edge, everywhere open to Prinsen. After a few thrusts in her cunt he turned his attention to his favourite hole, ramming his cock without preamble hard up her arse; it felt like a hot pole as it tore into her, and her back arched in pain against the table. His actions speeded up. He was ramming the full length of his cock in her, and she felt as if she was splitting in two down there; nothing but physical pain mingling with a terror which was nauseous as she realized that Gregory was not going to appear.

The ball of her thumb pressed so hard into the emerald that the flesh split, the green began to turn red. Streets away, the bleeper screeched to nobody.

Breathing harshly, the Dutchman gave a final, climatic heave and she felt his cum flooding in waves

210

into her arse. He shuddered, stood still with his black-hooded head thrown back for several moments, then he pulled his cock out of her and put it away, zipping himself up as he stared at her, his breathing gradually returning to normal. Then he said, stretching the words. 'I expect, Frannie, I expect you are thinking that so-called snuff movies don't actually *exist*.'

An icy hand squeezed at her heart and she gasped through her mouthful of knickers.

'But they do Frannie, oh yes indeed they do. There are not so many of them and there are, I understand, only two specialists in the making of that type of video. You are enjoying their company now – Ingram and John. They kill women on camera.'

The ceiling rushed away from her with sickening velocity as she fainted. But the relief was only momentary; the next thing she knew was the shock of cold water as a bucket of it was tipped over her face. She came to with a burning pain between her legs, cramps in her arms and thighs and a throat which, in the face of sheer terror, had tightened like a dried fig. The Dutchman was perched on the table at her side, facing her, hoodless. Ingram, still naked from the waist down, was now wearing the mask.

In Ingram's hands was an open, cut-throat razor.

Her thumb desperately found the emerald, she triggered another warning; but in the bar Gregory was staring into the empty glass in his hand, deciding that he would have another.

Prinsen said, 'You have heard of course, Lady Ballington, of the death of a thousand cuts? A pretty description. You are going to be doing your dying very slowly. I understand that it is the fancy of the afficionados of this type of film, who are paying a great deal of money for a copy, a very great deal, to witness much prolonged suffering before the victim' – he paused, showing his teeth – 'snuffs it. I myself am looking forward to enjoying the sight of much blood.'

He got off the table and sat on the arm of the sofa, saying, 'Okay, ready for action then, John, Ingram,' as Frannie's eyes rolled upwards until little but the whites showed and her teeth bit into the inside of her bottom lip. She began to tremble in convulsive spasms.

John moved in with the camera on his shoulder as Ingram laid the cold flat of his razor on the swell of Frannie's breast, just below the nipple. Her flesh shrank from it as a strangled cry came from Tony who picked up a chair and smashed at the smaller Ingram, he only succeeded in catching his shoulder but he did knock him off-balance.

Tony swung around, chair aloft, and started for the Dutchman but stopped half-way as a revolver, black silencer attached, appeared in Prinsen's hand.

'Foolish Tony. Please be putting the chair down.'

Tony took a long, deep breath, a mixture of anger and despair on his face as he lowered the chair. 'You didn't tell me about this, you bastard,' he said.

'Naturally. You would not have performed for us then, would you?' Prinsen snapped. 'Tie him please, John.'

Helpless, his hands secured behind him, Tony watched in horror as Ingram once again moved the razor towards Frannie's superb flesh and she screwed her eyes very tight.

In the bar, Gregory, lifting a fresh glass of beer to his lips, heard someone close by remark, 'Caddi out there was making a funny noise when I came in. Sounded as if the alarm was kind of half-going off.'

Gregory took one sip before the enormity of what he had heard registered, then, dropping the glass, he dived through the bar with a bellow, angered shouts following him as he fumbled with the lock of the Cadillac.

It felt like a warm, slow sting as Ingram nicked the

side of her breast with the end of his razor. Ingram stood back to admire his handiwork, John zoomed in on it and the Dutchman sighed and groped at his crotch. He went to Frannie and sharply slapped her cheek, making her eyes jerk open. He grinned. 'That first was for Danny. My friend here is going to cut you, and cut you, and cut you, all over, until you are dead,' he hissed.

From the depths of a hideous nightmare Frannie looked down at herself and when she saw her body with its spreading red stain she swooned again.

The blade was reaching for its second cut when Gregory burst through the frail outer door in an explosion of glass and wood. All of them except Frannie heard it and everything stopped.

The Dutchman aimed his revolver at the inner door and stood waiting for Gregory. But he made the fatal mistake of forgetting about Tony, standing near him with his hands tied, and when Gregory shouldered open the door, Tony charged into Prinsen, sending him staggering. The gun went off with a plop and the bullet shattered a china duck.

The furious fighting machine which was Gregory erupted among them. The Dutchman was dropped with a massive knee to the balls, and he collapsed doubled over to the floor. John was downed seconds later with a head-splitting blow with his camera and Ingram, tyring to get away, was felled as Gregory's two meaty hands, locked at the fingers, chopped viciously on the back of his neck, which snapped with a crack like a pistol shot.

Gregory stood above Ingram for several seconds, his eyes swivelling around the room as his chest rose and fell to the rasp of his breath, the power which the massive surge of adrenalin had given him making him look like a tank. Then he pulled out his flick knife and sliced through Tony's bonds, handing the knife to

Tony and nodding towards Frannie. As Tony freed her and Gregory examined the cut, unstuffing her knickers from her mouth and using them to staunch the flow of blood, Frannie recovered from her faint, her eyes opened and she wailed with an enormous relief at seeing Gregory. Then her shoulders convulsed and she began to sob.

Holding her knickers to his mistress's damaged breast, Gregory looked around at the havoc his entrance had brought. Ingram whose head was lying at an impossible angle was clearly dead. The Dutchman was writhing and moaning on the floor, still clutching between his legs. And John, the cameraman, lay very still on his back, breathing shallowly, blood from his cracked head forming a puddle on the floor.

As Tony put an arm around Frannie and comforted her, trying to stop her sobs, Gregory muttered, 'What the hell, Tony? What the bloody hell?'

'They were going to kill her. Revenge, for what happened in Amsterdam that night. A snuff movie.'

'Amsterdam? Snuff …?' Gregory's eyes opened wide as the implications of Tony's words became clear. He stared at the grovelling Dutchman. He had been in his leather gear and a mask the last time he had seen him, but Gregory recognized his shape. Slowly, he said, 'Lady Ballington, this was the one who caned you, wasn't it?'

She did not look. 'Yes,' she muttered.

'So.' Gregory's deadly fury, controlled, threatened to erupt again. But instead it imploded, formed in him a deadly, icy resolve. 'So. Who else knows about this house?'

'No one, as far as I know. They … they rented it in a false name, just for this.'

Something dawned on Gregory. Taking one of Frannie's hands he put it on her knickers against her breast, and took his away. 'Hold on to that,' he breathed as he reached for Tony's neck, took him by the throat and started to squeeze. 'You fucking well knew all the time, you worm, didn't you? You fucking well set her up, lured her here, didn't you? *Cunt!*'

Tony's breath was cut off, and he began to make choking noises as Gregory increased the pressure. 'You disgusting bastard. You fucking miserable, disgusting *bastard!*'

'For God's sake, Gregory, *No!* Stop it,' Frannie gasped. 'They threatened to *kill* him, he had no idea they planned this for me. Then he tried to save me.'

Slowly, very slowly, Gregory released his pressure, just as Tony's face began to shade into purple. Then he took his hands away, but disgust was on his face. 'Less than you deserve, my boy. Less than you deserve.'

'Christ. Oh, Jesus Christ,' Tony stammered as he gasped in air and rubbed his throat.

Gregory's resolve had not diminished. 'Here's what we have to do,' he said. He went to the chest of drawers, searched, found a linen serviette, and gave it to Frannie. 'Put this under your bra and get dressed, Lady Ballington. Keep a tight hold of that breast, I don't think it will bleed for long. There must absolutely be no doctor. Matilda will have to patch you up. Do it quickly, please. And as soon as we get back to the hotel you should prepare your pilot for an early take-off tomorrow. I'm taking no chances.'

By the time she was dressed Frannie had regained partial control of herself, but still the occasional sob escaped her lips. Gregory said, 'Take her out to the car, Tony. I'll join you in a minute.'

Alone with the two men and one corpse, Gregory picked up his flick-knife from where Tony had left it on the table and examined its blade while the Dutchman, veteran of the underworld, watched him with pain-filled eyes which recognized an icy intention.

Letting himself down on his haunches by Prinsen's

side he said, very quietly, 'By a supreme effort of will I let you off once before. This time there will be no reprieve.'

Several minutes later, in the hallway, the knife washed clean and back in his pocket, Gregory glanced through a telephone book and dialled a police number, studying the address on an envelope as his call was answered. He said, perfectly calmly, 'I want to report a death at 1311 West Haven Drive. There are also two badly injured men in the house. If you make it quick you might just be in time to save one from bleeding to death. He's had his balls cut off.'

Then Gregory hung up, strolled out to the Cadillac, and drove them all away.

# Home is the Huntress

What Gregory had done was brought rudely to my attention early the following morning when, still in my bed at the hotel, I switched on the television. In no mood for food I had ordered a glass of orange juice for breakfast, but when the screen lit up exactly at the beginning of a reportage of what was described as 'bloody carnage in downtown LA' I was transported once again into that dreadful house and I found that I could stomach only less than half a glass of that freshly pressed orange.

So, my faithful Gregory had castrated the Dutchman. But Prinsen would survive, I was informed by a frenetic reporter who seemed to regard the events in the house as something akin to an attack by the Manson tribe. John, the cameraman, I was informed, had a cracked skull and was in intensive care, in a condition regarded as critical, I was treated to a brief shot of him with tubes coming out of his nose and God-knew where else. Ingram was, of course, dead. There was much speculation about my blood-soaked Christian Dior knickers, about bloodstains on the tabletop, about neatly sliced pieces of rope. And my heart jumped when it was mentioned that the arc-lamps had been found switched on, and that there was a video camera on the floor. My image was on the film in that camera! I would be dragged into a horrible scandal! But the commentary continued with the fact that the camera had been discovered open, and there was no trace of the film. It had to have been Gregory's work. He seemed to have forgotten nothing except my knickers. Police were apparently working on the theory that some sort of sado-masochistic act had been in progress at the time of the attack, a fair, if understated assessment of the facts. They had even begun digging in the garden, looking for a body or bodies. The only man capable of speech, the Dutchman, was in a state of severe shock and had so far said nothing which amounted to more than garbled nonsense.

It seemed that, at least for the moment, we were safe.

I honestly did not know if I would have stopped Gregory had I known what he was about to do when Tony took me from what had been my intended place of violent death, but I shuddered to think that just maybe I would have let him get on with it, my only mitigation being that in any case I would have been most certainly powerless to prevent it.

Matilda came in to attend to my wound towards the end of the transmission. Thank God she did not connect the screened news with me. She was unusually quiet that morning, quite dreadfully shocked, poor thing. She had been told only half of the truth, that Gregory had rescued me from intended murder. The full story she was, of course, liable to discover from the media, but I wanted to protect her from it if I could.

I was not seriously damaged, and the weight of my breast tended to help hold the edges of the cut together. If I was lucky it would heal without leaving a scar. And I was mightily uncomfortable below, sore in my vagina from the Dutchman's nails, and in quite some pain in my poor, mistreated rectum which had bled during the rape and again during the night. But anyway, superficial wounds. How I had fared mentally, I had no idea.

As she finished dressing the cut, I noticed a tear rolling down Matilda's tubby cheek. Touched, a little surprised that she was so upset, I said, 'Don't cry for me, be happy. You have no idea what an emotion the gladness of being alive produces after staring death in the face.'

'How on earth can I be happy after what you've been subjected to?' she replied. 'The horror of it kept me awake half the night.'

I managed a smile. 'I'm sorry, Matilda. But it's over, it's all over. I'm all right and we're going home.'

'How can you possibly be all right?' Her four eyes flickered at me in disbelief.

'I don't know, but I think I am.' I sighed, then I swung my legs out of the bed, planting my feet firmly on the floor. 'One learns, I suppose.'

'*Learns*? Christ!' She actually sounded annoyed. 'You fucking well nearly get killed and all I hear is "one learns". Christ. Jesus *Christ*!'

Matilda.

We were due to take off for the first leg of the long trip back to England at ten am, but a heavy mist had rolled in from the sea and the flight was delayed for an hour and a half during which time I sat in, and paced the floor of, the VIP lounge, literally chewing my fingers, biting away at the cuticles in what I knew was an illogical display of nerves as I kept expecting the police to walk through the door at any moment and arrest our little party.

Gregory said not a word. He might have been a deaf mute. Doubtless he was experiencing the same apprehension as I. No, that's unfair, if we were to be implicated in the happenings at West Haven Drive, then I would be playing the part of one of the victims, Gregory the crazed killer. Matilda probably put our joint nervous behaviour down to the fact that we were suffering from the effects of shock – well, we must have been, as well, but that was not the half of it.

It was an enormous relief to be airborne. We were not free of America yet, but it felt like it.

Once we were aloft, and when I was finally able to think again, David popped into my head. This brought a lump to my throat as I realized that that was the first time my ravaged brain had had room for him since before getting in the car with Tony to go off to our 'party'. But I found myself thinking about him, about our incredible time together in Lanzarote, about our love for the first time with a sort of flat detachment. And, suddenly, in a moment which I welcomed with both relief and infinite sadness, I saw that I was trying to remember what my emotion of being helplessly in love had been like, and that it eluded me. It eluded me because it was not there any more. I was cured of David.

At what price? Well, two weeks of tremendous sexual indulgence had helped, that had been fine, that cost me nothing. But I considered that the events of the previous night, the sheer terror of it followed by a massive joy at being alive after all, emotions which seemed in the end to have swamped that passionate love for another being, they must have cost me something. And certainly Gregory would be paying a mental price. The dead man, the injured, they had paid too, but for them I had not the slightest grain of compassion. I sincerely hoped the one in intensive care would die too. Given the chance, I would pull out the tubes.

I decided to have a little chat with Gregory, a short while before our first refuelling stop at Chicago. Sitting beside him, resting my hand on his arm, I said, 'Gregory, I can't thank you enough for last night. I can't tell you how sorry I am about what I got you into.'

He kept staring straight ahead. 'Yes, ma'am,' he said. 'Look, if anything happens, if it should be traced to us, I want you to know that you can depend upon having the best lawyers in the world.'

'Thank you.' He tapped his jacket, over an inner pocket. 'I'm not too worried. This'll speak for me.'

I did not catch on. 'What will?'

'The video, Lady Ballington.' He looked at me then. I had never really noticed his eyes before. They were slate grey with good-humour creases around them. Today they wore a look of tired, sad, resignation. 'I doubt if any jury's going to convict me when they see that. When they see what was meant to happen to you.'

I was quite taken aback. For some reason I had assumed he would have destroyed the film. I said, 'Do you know if it came out?'

He stared at me for long moments, his expression unchanging. Finally, when I thought that he was declining to answer, he said, 'Oh yes. It came out all right. My lady.'

I don't recall my reply. I remember being very confused, mumbling some more apologies to the man and going forward to my seat. If Gregory had watched everything on that video, then he had seen my willing initial participation in that sordid little room, Tony undressing me while the others watched, me sucking Ingram's cock, getting screwed by him, over the sofa, on the floor, finally over that terrifying table where I was supposed to meet my end. For some reason I found that idea dreadfully embarrassing. Veteran as I was of porno photo sessions, of a totally abandoned sex film which would be seen by perhaps millions of people, the thought of my chauffeur/bodyguard sitting alone and watching my performance with those men, on his own, seemed more than embarrassing, it was downright sordid. Such, I thought, as I contemplated that fact, are the anomalies of the human mind.

I was glad to be home at Stratton Castle. Victor

greeted me with open arms which I tumbled gratefully into. We kissed, then he held me at arms' length and we studied each other. He was the same Victor, the healthy look of the well-heeled country squire who was rather more than a squire and rather more than well-heeled too. I did see his fifty-one years, though. I suppose that I had got so used to him before that I had stopped noticing his age. Now I saw him from a fresh point of view after nearly three months away. I liked what I saw; his years, I thought, hung well on him, they suited him.

But, clearly, something had happened to *me*, because the first words he spoke after that lengthy examination of me were, 'I do believe you seem to have been through quite a lot, my darling, darling Frannie.'

'It shows that much?' I replied, a little unhappy.

'No. Not much. But just a touch here.' He put a finger to the side of my eyes. 'And here.' He did the same thing to the corners of my lips. 'Nothing that doesn't do good things to you, though. That doesn't improve you, as if that were possible.' I smiled then, and he kissed my cheek. 'Your dimple's just as young as ever.'

My sexual adventures were at a close. I had no intentions of renewing them. I had ample records for Victor's enjoyment. I would relive my scene in New York with him, in Holland; we would have a copy of the videofilm in a while, and he already had the sex photos. Not an enormous collection perhaps, after three months' travels, but much of my time had been spent with my film-star lover and I most certainly had taken no film of *us* together. But there was no way I was going to see the video which was made that final night. Victor could, of course, and would – he would need to know how it had been – but I knew I would never be able to face the trauma of watching it together with him.

My vagina was still a touch sore, and my breast taped up but I needed above all to make love to my husband that night and we did and it was good and it was as it

222

should have been, my soreness went unnoticed through it. My most comfortable shoes were back on my feet.

I was home.

Three weeks have passed. Physically, I am completely healed. Amazingly, I think no lasting damage has been inflicted on my psyche either, despite the extra-ordinary things which occured to me during my three months of sexual holiday. No official knocks on the drawbridge of Stratton Castle either, so I imagine that the enquiries of the Californian police have led them nowhere. We have indulged, Victor and I, we have indulged luxuriantly, and our sex life seems stronger than ever. Matilda has, of course, joined in on two or three no-less-than-exquisite occasions.

We are one big happy family.

Having re-read what I wrote about my return home I find a piece where I stated that I had no intentions of renewing my sexual adventures. A little water has passed under the bridge since then.

And, of course, one gets restless, doesn't one?

F.

All Futura Books are available at your bookshop or
newsagent, or can be ordered from the following address
Futura Books, Cash Sales Department,
P.O. Box 11, Falmouth, Cornwall TR10 9EN.

Please send cheque or postal order (no currency), and
allow 60p for postage and packing for the first book
plus 25p for the second book and 15p for each additional
book ordered up to a maximum charge of £1.90 in U.K.

B.F.P.O. customers please allow 60p for
the first book, 25p for the second book plus 15p per
copy for the next 7 books, thereafter 9p per book

Overseas customers, including Eire, please allow £1.25
for postage and packing for the first book, 75p for the
second book and 28p for each subsequent title ordered.